"I have other plans for you," Ainsley said

The words were out before she quite realized how much they gave away.

Ivan lifted his eyebrows. "Now, that's an intriguing possibility."

She gave him a blithely mysterious smile, as if she wasn't frantically trying to figure out a way to cover her tracks. "I think so, too."

"Let's see…you need a burly hunk of man to move your furniture? Is that it?"

"It could be, but it isn't, although I can see where you'd want to picture yourself as the burly-hunk kind of furniture mover."

"I'll be happy to show you my muscles if you have any doubts about that."

He was teasing, she knew, but the image of him bare chested and flexing his biceps for her inspection brought a flush of heat to her cheeks again.…

Dear Reader,

Once in a while, a character appears in a bit part and winds up stealing the scene. In my last series, THE BILLION-DOLLAR BRADDOCKS, I intended Ainsley Danville to have only a walk-on role, but she charmed me into thinking she needed a story of her own. To my surprise, she wasn't satisfied with just one. She needed at least three in order to prove she could become an extraordinary matchmaker like her mentor, Ilsa Fairchild. And that's how this series, MATCHMAKER, MATCHMAKER, came to be written.

Harlequin American Romance novels are stories about home and family, about love, commitment and the belief that there is a happily ever after. *The Matchmaker's Apprentice* is no exception. I'm privileged to have spent the past year with Ainsley, and I hope you will love her enthusiasm for life as much as I do.

I appreciate the wonderful editors whose experience and insights make these books the best they can be. I appreciate the other writers of Harlequin American Romance novels who continue to raise the bar on quality. But most of all, I appreciate you, the reader. You're the reason books exist— you make it all worthwhile.

Thank you.

Karen Toller Whittenburg

Books by Karen Toller Whittenburg

HARLEQUIN AMERICAN ROMANCE
822—LAST-MINUTE MARRIAGE
877—HIS SHOTGUN PROPOSAL†
910—THE C.E.O.'S UNPLANNED PROPOSAL*
914—THE PLAYBOY'S OFFICE ROMANCE*
919—THE BLACKSHEEP'S ARRANGED MARRIAGE*

†The Texas Sheikhs
*The Billion-Dollar Braddocks

THE MATCHMAKER'S APPRENTICE
Karen Toller Whittenburg

HARLEQUIN®

TORONTO • NEW YORK • LONDON
AMSTERDAM • PARIS • SYDNEY • HAMBURG
STOCKHOLM • ATHENS • TOKYO • MILAN • MADRID
PRAGUE • WARSAW • BUDAPEST • AUCKLAND

ISBN 0-373-75010-2

THE MATCHMAKER'S APPRENTICE

Copyright © 2004 by Karen Whittenburg Crane.

Visit us at www.eHarlequin.com

Printed in U.S.A.

For Cindy and Cody
With best wishes for your own
Happily Ever After

Dear Diary,

It's finally happened. I've met the man I'm going to marry!

I'm in love!

Deeply. Passionately. Awesomely in love with Ivan Patrick Donovan.

Ivan Patrick Donovan.... Ivan. Ivan. Ivan.

It was love at first sight for him, too. I know it was!

It happened the very minute Matt introduced us tonight. Ivan smiled at me and my heart stopped. I mean, it really stopped! I could hardly breathe. He's so handsome! So tall! So gorgeous! His hair is blond, but darker than Miranda's honey blond. Not reddish-blond like Andrew's, either. And it's way darker than mine. Ivan's is like the sun...except deeper. Sort of brown, but with a lot of gold, too. His eyes are dark. Not black—that would be too ordinary, too...one-dimensional. They're like the color of winter midnights—dark and mysterious and... No, winter is too cold, too frozen, too blue to describe anything about him. His eyes are more like summer nights—misty and profound and…fiery. Fiery eyes. They blazed into my very soul!! He has passionate eyes…with hidden depths. And his voice—it sent shivers right through me! It's deep and husky—he could be on the radio if he wanted. But he's going to be a doctor. He told me. "I'm going to medical school," he said. Just like that. So confident. So positive. I told him I'm going to be an astronaut and he didn't laugh. Not like Matt and Miranda did when I told them. Ivan thinks I'm smart enough to be anything I want. He didn't say that, but I could see he believes I can do it if I want to. He shook my hand, too, like I was twenty instead of only thirteen. He smiled—did I mention how wonderful his smile is? He might have worn braces, but I don't think so because he has this one sort of crooked tooth. Just the tiniest bit of a slant…but it makes his smile seem really real. If you know what I mean. He is more handsome even than Matt, who is plenty handsome…for a brother. And his laugh is even nicer than Andrew's, who has the best laugh I know, even if he is my twin. Ivan acted all surprised and startled when he saw me. Well, really, I ran right into him. Andrew and me—I mean, Andrew and I—were skating in the ballroom and I was so determined to win I didn't know anybody was there and I skated right into Ivan. Kind of hard, too. But he just laughed. Matt scolded me for not watching what I was doing, but Ivan smiled at me and I knew he didn't think I was just a silly kid.

I think that's when I fell in love, but it wasn't until Ivan said, "You're Ainsley? Matt's little sister, Ainsley? The way he talks about you, I was expecting an adorable little toddler, not a beautiful, young lady. Shame on you, Matt, for not warning me your baby sister is already a heartbreaker," that I knew for certain. Me? A heartbreaker? I could have died!! My heart, my soul, my whole being just melted!! He talked to me all through dinner, too, pretending he didn't know which fork to use or which glass and stuff like that. He said it was because he grew up on a farm and they didn't have fancy dinners, but he was only being funny. And he liked talking to me. I could tell. And it didn't make any difference that he's older than me. Or that he's in college and I'm only in seventh grade. Our hearts were made to beat as one. It's like we knew each other in another life! And when I had to go upstairs to do my homework—I'll never forgive Miranda for being so bossy!!!—Ivan said in his deep, wonderful voice, "I can't tell you how glad I am finally to have met you, Ainsley." Finally. He said it just like that. Like he knew it was our destiny to meet. Like he'd expected us to fall in love at first sight. Like it was kismet or something. Like he recognized that I was his destiny, just as I know he is mine.

I hope he comes home with Matt next weekend, too.

And every weekend from now on. By the time they graduate from college, I'll be almost sixteen. Old enough to date. Old enough to be taken seriously. Old enough to marry Ivan and live happily ever after! Forever and ever and ever....

Mrs. Ivan Donovan.   Ainsley Elizabeth Donovan.
Ainsley Danville Donovan.
Ainsley loves Ivan.   Ivan loves Ainsley.
Ainsley and Ivan forever.

October 31
Dear Diary,
I can't believe I just found this old diary again. And on Halloween, too! Spooky, huh? I thought I'd lost it forever, but there it was in my closet, stuck in that stupid Cinderella backpack I used to carry in junior high. I can't believe I was such a total airhead back then. Cinderella!!! Can you believe I was ever so drop-dead dumber than dumb? The backpack was probably Miranda's idea of a great birthday gift. Or Matt's. They'd like to think of me as a little girl forever and ever and ever. They hate the fact that I'm a grown-up. But I'm in high school now and Andrew and I will be fifteen on our next birthday. Sooner or later, Miranda and Matt will have to stop treating me like such a baby. They don't do that to Andrew…and he's only an hour and twenty minutes older than me. When he says he's going to be a professional photographer, they fall all over themselves to encourage

him. Of course, he's talented. I'm not saying he isn't or that he shouldn't be a photographer because he'll be really, really good at that. I'm his twin. I know these things. It's just that when I say I've decided I'm going to be a professional matchmaker everybody just laughs and reminds me that I said I wanted to be an astronaut when I was thirteen and an engineer when I was eleven, and a fairy godmother when I was six. Miranda likes to points out that I'm not really suited to any of those positions, although a lot she knows about it. I could be suited to be an engineer or an astronaut if I wanted to. But I want to be a matchmaker! Which is the same as a fairy godmother, when you think about it, and that's what I've really always wanted to be. I just said I wanted to be other things so Matt and Miranda wouldn't tease me, so they'd encourage me like they do Andrew. But they never take me seriously, no matter what I do. And the thing is, I know I'll be good at being a matchmaker. I just know it! Matt says I shouldn't worry about a career, that I'll have plenty of time to decide once I get to college. I'm not even sure I want to go to college. I already know the important things about being a matchmaker. I believe in Love and Romance and Happily Ever After. All my friends ask me for advice about their romantic interests. I'm good at giving advice. I really, really am. I'll be a great matchmaker and someday I'll have my own office—with a view— and the business will be called F.G. (short for Fairy

Godmother, except I won't tell Miranda and Matt what it stands for!) Matchmaking. Then they'll think twice about calling me "Baby." Ugh.

I used to be able to talk to Ivan about stuff like this, but he's gotten so serious since he's in med school and he never has time to play Ping-Pong with me when he does come to Danfair...which is not very often anymore. I don't know why I thought I was in love with him, anyway. He's just like a brother and teases me almost as much as Matt and Andrew. And he looks at Miranda like she's ice cream. Maybe I'll make them my first assignment as a matchmaker. Ivan and Miranda. Ha! It would serve them right if I got them together and they ended up married. Then they'd have to stop teasing me about wanting to be Cinderella's fairy godmother. Then they'd have to admit I know what I'm doing. Then I'll find somebody for Matt and he'll have to admit I'm a good matchmaker. And Andrew...well, he is my twin. He may not need much help.

Oops, gotta go. A whole group of us are going trick-or-treating and then to a party at Sabrina's house and I think Collier might try to kiss me tonight. I haven't decided yet if I'll let him. I'm off....

P.S. Don't get lost again, okay?

Chapter One

Discretion was not Ainsley Danville's strong suit.

Which was why she was standing at the back of the Newport Presbyterian Church—the second of three bridesmaids who were all wearing silky poufs of lavender organza—and waiting for the wedding co-ordinator to cue her entrance. Ahead of her, a bower of roses lined the doorway like a dowager's perfume, thick and thorny with fragrance. Pachelbel's "Canon in D" gushed from the pipe organ in a waterfall of chords, beckoning the bridesmaids forward and down the aisle. The flames of a hundred candles lent an eerie glow to the dark interior of the old church, lighting a sure path to disaster.

Ainsley clenched the nosegay of pink rosebuds in her hands and watched as her elder sister, Miranda, the first bridesmaid, started down the aisle. Ainsley craned her neck to catch a glimpse of the groom. If he had any sense, he'd be halfway to Canada by now. But no. There he was, her cousin Scott, looking slightly less geeky than usual, so hopeful and eager to see Molly, his bride, it was heartrending. He was about to make a terrible mistake. Ainsley knew it in the depths of her matchmaker's soul. And it was her fault.

She had wanted to be a matchmaker for as long as she could remember. Well, actually, she'd started out wanting to be everyone's fairy godmother. While other little girls dreamed of being Cinderella, Ainsley had practiced waving her sparkly plastic wand and sending the transformed Ella off to the ball, where she would meet the man of her dreams…a prince who would fall madly, instantly in love because he'd been cunningly placed in her path by her wise fairy godmother. That was the way happily ever afters *really* happened.

Ainsley had suspected it for years, long before she began reading everything—nonfiction, fiction, biographies, cultural histories—anything with even a slight relevance to the art of courtship and marriages. She'd weathered her family's teasing and a lot of snickering from friends. But a matchmaker is what she wanted to be and, as if her own fairy godmother had arranged it, she had discovered a mentor in Ilsa Fairchild of IF Enterprises, an elite, very selective matchmaking service located in Providence. Just a hop, skip and jump from Newport. Ainsley had invested her considerable energy into lobbying for a position at IF, and to everyone's amazement—even a little to her own surprise—Ilsa had taken her on as an apprentice.

Ainsley couldn't have been more excited. Or more enthusiastic. Finally, she was going to have a career of her own. Finally, she was going to be a bona fide matchmaker. Finally, her overprotective brothers and sister would have to stop treating her like a baby and admit she was capable of so much more than being "cute." The position with IF Enterprises was perfect in every way and it suited her to a tee.

Except for her ongoing struggle to keep a lid on her enthusiasm.

If only she'd been discreet and told people her job was in personal relations, as Ilsa had advised her to do. If only she hadn't informed the family, *bragged,* in fact, that she'd taken an apprenticeship with the most exclusive matchmaker in New England. If only she'd kept her mouth shut about IF Enterprises and her dream-come-true job, then she wouldn't be standing at the back of a church right now watching her cousin prepare to marry the wrong woman.

"Ainsley...?" The wedding coordinator—a largish woman in a purple smock—hissed at her to get her attention. "You're next. Remember...left foot first. Count your steps just as we practiced."

But Ainsley had no recollection of last night's rehearsal. She'd been too busy trying to think of some way to sabotage the wedding and stop the marriage from taking place. Obviously, no good plan had occurred to her because here she was, about to imitate the rhythmic steps that had taken Miranda three-quarters of the way to the altar already.

Miranda had paid attention last night.

Miranda always paid attention.

Miranda did everything to perfection. If she'd wanted to stop this wedding, none of them would be here now.

"Ainsley!" The coordinator hissed at her again, propelling her under the rose bower with a firm hand on the back of the organza bustle. Ainsley nearly stumbled, but caught herself and took the first fateful step—with her right foot. "Left foot!" The coordinator's whispered reminder had her switching rhythm in midstride and coming even closer to losing her balance. If she'd thought that falling flat on her face would do anything more than merely delay the bride's entrance, she'd go sprawling here and now. She looked back over her shoulder and saw Molly, in her bridal white, hovering in the bride's room doorway, looking excruciatingly nervous, but committed.

So the marriage was going to take place, despite Ainsley's misgivings. She'd done all she could, had said as much as she dared, had hinted at her doubts—as a professional and a loving cousin—to both Scott and Molly with no results. She hadn't confessed her part in the matchmaking, but she had tried to explain her concern to her siblings. As the three of them typically did, they'd discounted her qualms and assured her there was nothing to worry about. Scott and Molly were perfect for each other. Two peas in a pod. Two nuts in a shell. Two bugs in a bottle.

Which, of course, was the problem.

There was nothing for it now, but to hope they would have a brighter future than she could imagine for them. So as the music swelled around her, Ainsley put a smile on her face and did her own version of the bridesmaid's shuffle—step-pause, step-pause— letting her hips sway just a little under the yards of shimmering lavender organza.

Miranda, who looked stunning as always, had reached the front and was making her final turn. Eldest brother Matt was standing tall and straight next to Scott. He smiled encouragingly at Ainsley as she reached the midway point. Andrew, Ainsley's twin, stood next to Matt, looking handsome, but uncomfortable in his tuxedo. He winked at her and her heart sank all over again. Even Andrew didn't understand why this match was so wrong or why she was so worried about it.

But no one would listen to her and now it was too late. It had been too late from the minute she'd set up that first, disastrous *introduction of possibilities* for Scott. Or more probably, it had been too late from the moment she'd confided excitedly to him that she was working for IF Enterprises and he'd asked her, *begged* her, to set up a match for him.

And she had.

Despite Ilsa's cautioning her from the start that she needed to learn some basic tenets of matchmaking before taking on any clients. Despite knowing on one level or another that she was acting on impulse as much as intuition. She'd been certain, though, that she knew the right woman for Scott. Bubbly, extroverted and warm, Shelby would have been the perfect foil for Scott's shy, introverted and intellectual self. Ainsley had been positive that once the two met, the result would be an instantaneous attraction and a match truly made in heaven.

And she hadn't necessarily been wrong. Just unfortunate in where she'd set up that initial meeting. A bit unlucky with the timing, and tardy in stepping forward to rectify the mistake. Scott wound up at the wrong table in the restaurant and, within an hour, was head over heels in love with a quiet mouse of a woman named Molly…instead of meeting Shelby as Ainsley had intended.

Two unbelievably short months later, here they were, Scott and Molly, about to be married.

Two-thirds of the way down the aisle, Ainsley realized how few guests had actually shown up to witness the ceremony. Of course, there'd never been any question of the wedding being anything other than small. Molly didn't have family, except for her ancient Aunt Beatrice, who was too elderly to travel but who'd sent the couple an enormous soup tureen shaped like a swan. Even Miranda had wondered aloud what use Molly and Scott would have for a soup tureen, since neither of them had any friends. Well, at least, not any close friends, which was why the bridal party consisted of Scott's four cousins and his two younger sisters.

Another reason this match was all wrong, Ainsley decided as she reached the front and made her final turn, was that the bridal party was out of balance. There was one more bridesmaid than groomsmen. Miranda had tried to fix the problem because she disliked odd numbers, but Scott's father—who wasn't that happy about the wedding to begin with—had declared quite firmly that he wasn't paying for some stranger's tuxedo just to even out the bridal party. Scott had said he didn't care, and Molly had agreed because she and Scott agreed about everything.

Which was the main reason this marriage was a bad idea.

Two people shouldn't expect to be everything to each other. But Molly and Scott seemed to believe it was possible...and perfect. Neither of them possessed much in the way of social graces, so there was little hope either of them would expand the social circle of the other. They were both shy. Both inhibited and unassertive. Between them, they possessed barely an ounce of backbone.

Scott and Molly had too much in common. Ainsley could see that very clearly. While she wouldn't go so far as to predict that happiness was an impossibility for them, she could not believe it was very likely, either. They'd grow bored with each other, stifled in the narrowness of their lives.

Ainsley was only an apprentice matchmaker, but she knew there was a reason opposites attract. She understood that familiarity could, and often did, breed contempt. It didn't take a rocket scientist to figure out that this marriage wouldn't set the world on fire...or, more important, either one of its counterparts. But no one other than Ainsley seemed concerned.

Then again, she was the only one who knew what a mismatch she'd inadvertently put together. She was the only one who felt guilty for bringing about this ill-fated romance.

Emily, the older of Scott's two sisters and still young enough to consider her curly red hair a curse, looked worried as she reached the end of the aisle. ''Molly tore her dress,'' she said to Ainsley in a whispered aside as she stepped into the maid of honor's place. ''She stepped on her train.''

A bad sign.

Ainsley looked toward the entrance, where Claire, Scott's baby sister, was starting her walk down the aisle, scattering rose petals over the carpet. Claire was also a redhead and, at eleven, too old really for the role she was fulfilling with such exaggerated care...dropping two petals on this side, three petals on that side. Molly had wanted a flower girl and there was no one else. The ring bearer—Molly had wanted one of those, too—had been easier to find. They'd borrowed Calvin Braddock, the five-year-old son of Bryce and Lara Braddock, who, if not close friends of either Scott or Molly, were at least considered friends of the Danville family. Ainsley could see Cal's white-blond cowlick darting back and forth behind the purple smock of the wedding coordinator, who seemed to be trying to keep the boy from dashing down the aisle.

The music was too loud at the front of the church to hear what was happening at the back. Ainsley was surprised to see a sudden collective stir of activity. The congregation—at least, the dozen or so Danville relatives seated in the first few rows—grew restless and began turning around in the pews to see what was going on. Even Scott, who'd spent the entire processional so far staring anxiously at his shoes, looked up.

"I got to tell the groom somethin'!" Calvin's little-boy voice broke through the lull between the final chords of Pachelbel and the opening chimes of Wagner's "Bridal Chorus." "She told me to tell him!"

Cal pulled free of the wedding coordinator's grasping hands and ran, tuxedo tails flying, down the aisle, dashing past Claire in a move that knocked her off her feet and scattered her rose petals in one thick, damp clump. "She 'loped!" Calvin shouted as he caught sight of Scott at the altar. "The bride 'loped!"

Scott went pale with alarm, but it was Matt who

moved forward to calm the ring bearer and ask for a more coherent explanation.

"Catch your breath, Calvin," Matt said soothingly. "And start from the beginning."

Cal obediently sucked in a huge gasp of air, his bright gaze darting toward Scott. "Miss Molly," he said in a rush. "She told me to tell you she's sorry, but she 'loped."

"Eloped?" Matt questioned, articulating the word carefully. "Are you saying that Molly eloped?"

Confirming the interpretation with a vigorous nod, Calvin repeated the message excitedly. "She 'loped with Mad Mack in the Mackmobile."

SITTING ON A LOW RISER under the bridal bower, Ainsley plucked at the pouf of organza bunched around her like a lavender nest and felt guiltier by the second. Calvin's startling announcement still reverberated in the church sanctuary, picked up by one person after another after another, repeated in a confusing hum of overlapping voices.

She eloped? With a cartoon character?

Mad Mack? Are you sure *that's what he said?*

She must've had an emergency. Why else would she run off like that?

He said Mad Mack, I'm telling you.

How can the bride have eloped if the groom's still standing up there?

Mad Mack? The bride eloped with someone called Mad Mack?

That's the most ridiculous thing I've ever heard.

The bridal party of sisters and cousins had stood restlessly for a few awkward moments, not knowing where to look or what to do. Then, one by one, they settled on the altar steps or found a seat in the front pews. And there they sat, awaiting instruction or dismissal, without a clue as to what action—if any— might be appropriate. Matt, being the oldest of the cousins and the best man, had immediately gone to the back of the church, where he could be seen firing brusque questions at Phyllis while he paced from the vestibule doorway to the empty bride's room and then outside to the front church steps, where he stared at the street. Inside the sanctuary, the clatter of conversation rose and fell in hushed waves. Whispered questions quickly took on an indignant tone and grew louder, becoming quietly outraged that anyone—especially a woman without connections, or much in the way of beauty, brains or personality to recommend her—would offer such an insult to Scott Danville. The entire Danville family, for that matter. Every wedding guest present was, after all, either a member of the Danville clan or a close friend of the family since Molly came, basically, unencumbered with kith or kin.

The clamor stuttered suddenly into a moment's awkward pause just in time for everyone to hear Uncle Edward's vehement instruction to his son. "Forget it. You are *not* going after her, Scott. She just jilted you, for heaven's sake. You! A Danville. Clearly, the woman is insane. You can't possibly want her back even if you knew how to find her, which you don't, and which I wouldn't let you do, if you did. She's gone," he said angrily. "And I say, good riddance!"

Ainsley glanced down the riser to watch Scott, flushed with humiliation, hurt and anger, give up the struggle like a balloon with a slow leak. She knew the moment the reality hit him full in the heart— *Molly was gone!*—and he sank like a stone to sit, slumped and stunned, with his head in his hands, devastated, desolate and without a shred of hope to hold on to. In her whole life, Ainsley had never seen more eloquent body language. Even his vividly red hair seemed to have lost its light and become nothing more than a listless covering on his head.

This was her fault. Ainsley knew it all the way to the tips of her lavender-painted toenails. She didn't want to admit it, didn't want to see herself as the spoiler, but there it was. Molly's baffling departure wasn't quite so much of a mystery to Ainsley as it was to everyone else. Unexpected and surprising? Yes. In a million years, Ainsley wouldn't have predicted Molly's last-minute dash from the church. But now that it had happened…?

Well, she could think of a possible explanation, a plausible, probable interpretation, one glaring moment at last night's rehearsal dinner when the apprentice matchmaker had, once again, forgotten the importance of discretion and opened her mouth before engaging her brain.

Obviously, she was still several lessons short of being the prudent, discerning matchmaker she wanted, and was determined, to become.

"I realize this joyous occasion has taken a somber turn, Ains, but you look unaccountably gloomy. What gives?" Handsome as a god, with a smile that quite simply made the world a brighter place, Andrew dropped down to sit beside her, bustling the yards of organza out of his way and fixing her with a persistent, you-may-as-well-tell-me look.

But Ainsley couldn't confess. Not yet. Not even to her trusted twin. "In case you haven't noticed, our cousin is devastated."

"Can't argue with you there. But since you were completely convinced Scott was marrying the wrong woman anyway, I thought you might see this as some form of divine intervention. Even if it is a little difficult to envision Mad Mack in the *deus ex machina* role."

"I never even heard of Mad Mack," she said with a sigh. "Much less a Mackmobile."

"You should spend more time watching cartoons," Andrew suggested. "Mad Mack is a part-man, part-machine superhero and the Mackmobile is the coolest car on television. Well, at least it's the coolest *animated* car on the Cartoon Stars channel.''

"You obviously have too much time on your hands.''

"Me and Calvin,'' he agreed. "He's five and I'm still five at heart.''

Ainsley offered a frown, although she adored her twin for trying to cheer her up with his silliness. "I feel awful about this, Drew. Even though I never thought Molly and Scott were a match made in heaven, I never wanted him to suffer. Especially not because of me and my big mouth.''

"You do not have a big mouth.'' Andrew slipped an arm around her shoulder and gave her an affectionate squeeze. "Your tongue may run like an outboard motor at times, but proportionally, your mouth is the perfect size for your face.''

She nudged him with her elbow. "This is serious, Andrew. Don't make jokes.''

"I can't help myself, Ainsley. The bride eloped with Mad Mack. That's a little difficult to take seriously.''

"Try,'' she urged him, although truthfully, she wished she could see the humor in the situation. Any humor at all.

"Okay,'' he said, "but I can't promise a non-serious remark won't slip out from time to time.''

"Just so it doesn't happen here and now or any time Scott is around.''

He nodded, rested his forearms on his knees, clasped his hands together and let the resulting loose knot of fingers rock up and down, up and down, as he contemplated the here and now. "Do you think we'll still get to have the wedding feast?"

She lifted an eyebrow. "I imagine dinner will be canceled." He opened his mouth, but she cut him off. "And, please, don't ask Uncle Edward if you can make yourself a plate for later."

"Seems a shame to waste all that food. And the wedding cake. Maybe I should take the cake to the studio, take a few pictures for the old Danville scrapbook."

She lifted the other eyebrow and he went back to contemplating. "No, you're wrong, Ainsley. Uncle Edward won't cancel dinner. He'll want to finish the day on an up note."

"As opposed to a sour note?"

"As opposed to letting a part-man, part-machine superhero triumph over a Danville. You know, I always thought there was a hint of Bad Belle in Molly."

"*Bad Belle?* Let me guess. She's Mad Mack's girlfriend?"

"Good guess. Imagine a bosomy brunette with super powers and a big black motorcycle."

"I'm never letting my kids watch cartoons," Ainsley said.

"Too bad we can't put Scott in front of the television now. A little time with Bad Belle and he'd feel a lot better.''

"That's not funny. And even if a stupid cartoon could make him feel better, it won't make me feel one bit less guilty."

"Oh, come on, Ains. This isn't your fault. You can never really know the truth of what's inside another person. There's no way you could have guessed Molly would rather take a ride in the Mackmobile than get married today."

Ainsley caught the advice in his teasing, knew he was telling her she couldn't take the blame for today's events. Her siblings, and especially her twin, had always been right there when something in her life went awry, ready with assurances that she—the angelically cute baby of the family—wasn't at fault, shouldn't feel guilty, couldn't truly be to blame for whatever had happened.

But she wasn't a baby anymore. Despite her family's reluctance to allow her to grow up, she had. She was, whether they wanted to believe it or not, an adult. And she had no intention of absolving herself from the guilt she rightfully felt. She hadn't wanted Scott and Molly to marry. She still thought she was right about their chances of finding true happiness together. But she hadn't wanted her beliefs to cause them unhappiness, either.

She deserved a hefty chunk of responsibility for today's fiasco and she deserved to feel gloomy that her first attempt at matchmaking had been a complete and utter disaster.

Andrew, however, would never allow her to admit her guilt to him, so she tapped his arm with her bridesmaid's bouquet. "Let's talk about something else. Tell me about your date."

"What date?"

"Your date to the wedding. Jocelyn? A petite brunette? In a pink dress? Where did you put her?" She glanced out at the pool of somber faces, looking for the young woman Andrew had introduced earlier as his date.

"Fifth row, left. In the middle." He glanced in the general vicinity of the brunette and smiled. "I'd go sit with her, but she's wearing pink and you know how that clashes with my hair."

He was the only redhead in their branch of the family and his hair was, in Ainsley's prejudiced opinion, his second-best feature. It was strawberry-blond, a rich reddish-gold, and thick, with just enough curl to give it great body and texture, and just enough length to identify him as a nonconformist. He didn't have freckles or the pale, ivory skin of most redheads, either, and his athletic, outdoor tan was a perfect foil for the blue, Danville eyes…Andrew's best feature of all. He was better looking than Matt, although not technically as handsome. Ainsley, being his twin, might have been slightly prejudiced in his favor, but as she adored both of her brothers, she couldn't imagine it made much difference either way.

"Do you ever think about getting married, Drew?" she asked, his pet name giving the question a serious lilt and the expectation of a truthful answer.

"Good grief, no," he said, sounding at least seventy-five percent honest. "I'm planning to live a long, happy life."

She laughed under her breath. "Marriage increases a man's lifespan by a good ten or fifteen years. Didn't you know that?"

"I said 'long, *happy* life.' There's a difference. Besides, even if I was inclined toward a monogamous, committed relationship, where would I find a woman who'd willingly put up with my nomadic schedule?"

"Maybe if you dated someone more than once or twice, you'd come closer to finding someone who keeps as weird a schedule as you do." He was always off chasing photographs, leaving on the spur of the moment, staying gone until he was ready to come home, getting up at dawn to catch the perfect angle of light, camping out for a month, waiting for the full moon or no moon or a sliver of moon or some distant star—whatever he needed in the picture he'd visualized in his head. "Maybe you ought to try dating another photographer."

He grinned. "Not interested. It's all I can do to get along with my photography assistants, and you and I both know they only tolerate my artistic temperament because I pay them big bucks to do it. I'm looking for a new assistant, by the way.''

''I thought you just hired one.''

He shrugged. ''She left before lunch on her first day of work.''

''Maybe you should hire male assistants.''

''I have. I'm an equal opportunity employer, but it's mostly females who answer my ads. Consequently, I usually have a female assistant.''

''Do you want me to find someone for you?''

''I don't think so, Miss Matchmaker.''

''Apprentice,'' she corrected. ''I'm only the matchmaker's apprentice.'' Obviously not a very good one, either.

''All the more reason for me to advertise for an assistant in the newspaper. No offense, Ains, but you'd hook me up with some romantically inclined Cinderella and I'd have to fire her for mooning over me instead of doing what needs to be done. Don't give my lack of an assistant another thought. Please.''

She'd never set up an *introduction of possibilities* for Andrew and some ''romantically inclined Cinderella.'' She might make her share of mistakes, but she wouldn't make that one. ''All right,'' she agreed with a smile. ''I'll keep my recommendations to myself.'' She nodded toward the fifth row, left, in the middle. ''Go talk to your date. She's starting to look neglected.''

He stood, believing he'd fulfilled his mission of

cheering up his twin sister. "I think I'll show her the exit and see if I can interest her in dressing up as superheroes for the duration of the evening. She'd look good in one of those outfits, don't you think?"

Ainsley pretended to consider. "As long as the color doesn't clash with your hair."

Just then, Uncle Edward stepped up onto the dais and cleared his throat. "Thank you all for waiting," he said. "And thank you for your support today. While I can't ask you to join us for the celebratory reception originally planned, I'm extending a heartfelt invitation for each of you to join us for dinner and dancing and whatever else we decide to do in order to put aside our—" he glanced down at Scott's defeated and despondent slump "—disappointment." Then, gesturing toward the doors, Uncle Edward bent down and offered his son a comforting pat on the shoulder.

Andrew looked at Ainsley. "See you at the buffet tables," he said and walked over to offer Scott a few words of encouragement before heading for the fifth row, left, and Jocelyn, who welcomed his approach with a wide smile and a tinge of pink blush on her cheeks.

And for probably the first time since Ainsley had become the matchmaker's apprentice, the possibility of a romantic match didn't even cross her mind.

Chapter Two

"Molly left Scott waiting at the altar and eloped with a cartoon character?"

The way Ilsa phrased it, the way her voice modulated the question into a simple inquiry, didn't make Ainsley feel any better. If anything, having to relate the whole sorry story on a sunny Monday morning while sitting in Ilsa's elegant office made it seem a thousand times worse. "It wasn't really Mad Mack." Ainsley stopped, realizing how ridiculous that sounded. "But, of course, you know that."

Ilsa was patient—a trait Ainsley had run up against numerous times since she'd begun her apprenticeship six months ago—and she simply folded her hands on top of the polished cherrywood desk and waited.

Ainsley began again. "What we know is that Molly bolted out the front doors, jumped into a black sports car—which must have looked like the Mackmobile to Calvin—and was gone. Phyllis—she's the wedding coordinator for the church—was so upset. She's never had a bride elope before. At least not with someone other than the groom.''

''Molly didn't leave a note?''

Ainsley shook her head. ''No, and if she was having doubts, Scott didn't have a clue. But then he never does.'' Ainsley made a face. ''He's my cousin and I'm awfully fond of him, but he's never been adept at reading emotions. Not even his own.''

''This must have been quite a shock to him.''

''He's convinced himself she ran away with some guy who was a bartender at the restaurant where they met. Where Scott and Molly met, I mean. But I can't really see her striking up a conversation with a bartender, much less running away with him.''

''It does seem an unlikely scenario,'' Ilsa acknowledged. ''On the other hand, IF Enterprises deals in possibilities and it's been my experience that what seems impossible is sometimes exactly what happens. What I find more interesting is why she decided not to marry Scott…and why at the very last minute. The way you've described her, that does seem out of character.''

''It was my fault,'' Ainsley said, blurting out her guilt in a rush and without an ounce of forethought. ''It's all my fault.''

Ilsa smiled. ''How could Molly's decision be *your* fault?''

Ainsley hadn't meant to confess. When she'd walked into the office this morning, she'd had no inclination to own up to her part in the wedding fiasco. She didn't want Ilsa to be disappointed in her, for one thing. She didn't want to get fired, for another. But mostly, she didn't want anyone else telling her she wasn't responsible when she knew in her heart she was. "I set up the match," she said, unable to prevent the misery of the past two days from welling up in her voice. "I know I wasn't supposed to do any matchmaking until you gave me the okay. I know I'm only an apprentice and that I haven't learned everything I need to before I start taking clients. But Scott's a cousin. I didn't think of him as a *real* client."

She paused, briefly hoping Ilsa would just fire her on the spot so she wouldn't have to confide the rest, but Ilsa didn't say a word. "It was more like a…a favor," Ainsley continued, feeling the words doubling up on her tongue, knowing she talked too much, too fast, when she was nervous. But there were mitigating circumstances in this case and she wanted Ilsa to understand. "I never meant to tell anyone—well, no one other than Miranda and my brothers—that you'd hired me as your apprentice, but with Scott, it just sort of slipped out. He pestered me about finding a match, begged me to set him up with someone who might want to have a relationship with him. He has a wonderful heart, but on the surface he's your ordinary goofy, geeky type, the kind of guy women never give a second glance. I doubt he's had more than a dozen dates in his entire life…and he's nearly thirty."

"Self-conscious, ill-at-ease, lacks confidence and consequently tries too hard." Ilsa nodded. She understood the problems of a lonely heart.

"Yes," Ainsley agreed, latching onto the sympathetic image. "On top of that, he's never figured out how to handle social situations with any polish, so he routinely avoids them and spends way too much of his time in his lab studying the mating habits of bugs...or something equally unromantic and boring. His work is practically all he ever talks about, though, so when he pleaded with me to set up an *introduction of possibilities* for him, I couldn't say no."

"Naturally, you wanted to help your cousin."

"Yes, and I just happened to know the perfect woman for him. You know Shelby Stewart, right? Well, she is exactly what Scott needs. She's bubbly, fun and very different from him. Her personality would be such a complement to his. She'd bring out his sense of humor—he honestly does have one—and force him into social situations where he'd have to pull himself together. She'd put some sparkle in his life, and Scott is exactly the sort of man she needs, too. He'd help her organize her life—she's been something of a wild child, you know—and provide her with some stability. He'd be good for her. She'd be good for him. They'd be good together. I just knew in my heart they'd be a perfect match."

Ilsa's expression remained interested, but neutral, so Ainsley stopped trying to justify her reasoning and rushed on with her confession. "To make a long story short, I set up a 'chance' encounter a couple of months ago. On Valentine's Day. Except somehow, Scott wound up at the wrong table and met Molly by mistake. It was a fluke. Wrong place, wrong time, wrong table, wrong match…and it's all my fault. If it hadn't been for me, Scott would never have gone anywhere near The Torrid Tomato—it's not his kind of place, at all. Too trendy and fun, if you know what I mean."

An arching of eyebrows indicated Ilsa did know the place and what Ainsley meant.

"The truth is, Scott would never have been there if I hadn't set up that *introduction of possibilities* with Shelby. He'd certainly never have noticed Molly if I hadn't told him to keep an eye out for opportunity as he walked in. I wanted him to be thinking about something other than how uncomfortable he felt, you see, but I guess he took that to mean he was supposed to come in and start looking for Ms. Right. I don't know what he was thinking. He was supposed to see me and come straight over to where I was sitting with Shelby. Then I was going to make an excuse to slip away for a couple of minutes and let them get acquainted. But he walked through the door and zeroed in on Molly, who was sitting all alone at a table for two back in the far corner. I still don't know how he happened to see her, much less why he decided to walk over and introduce himself. I mean, he's not normally brave. And I don't know how she happened to catch his eye. She's so shy and quiet, so timid and reserved...so much like Scott. Who would have imagined she'd invite him to join her for dinner? Or that he'd propose to her only a couple of days later?'' Ainsley paused, knowing even as the words left her mouth that she should have imagined at least the possibility of something going awry. A good matchmaker would have thought out more than one scenario before she ever set up the initial encounter.

But she hadn't.

The silence stretched and Ainsley finally forced her eyes up to meet Ilsa's, made herself look for the censure she was sure she'd find.

Ilsa's expression reflected only a thoughtful curiosity.

"You warned me to be cautious," Ainsley said. "You told me to learn the basics, to be patient. But I completely ignored your advice because I was so *certain* Scott and Shelby would hit it off...and now it's all a big mess. Scott is devastated. The whole Danville family is in an uproar. Uncle Edward has declared Molly will never be welcome in his home, so even when—*if*—she comes back, Scott won't be able to forgive her without upsetting everyone all over again. It's an awful situation and it's all my fault."

Ilsa, a master at interpreting even the slightest slip of the tongue, sat quietly for a moment. "Do you know why Molly ran away from her wedding, Ainsley?''

Time to face the consequences and divulge the worst truth of all. ''She ran away because I said she was the wrong match for Scott.''

Ilsa blinked. ''You *said* that to her?''

''Not those exact words.'' Ainsley felt sick with regret. ''And I said it to everyone present at the time, not directly to her.''

''When did this happen?''

''At the wedding rehearsal Friday night.''

''You told a couple, in front of their family and friends, and on the day before their wedding, that you considered their match a mistake?'' Now there was astonishment in her voice, a startled surprise, a hint of dismay even her refinement couldn't disguise. ''Why would you do that, Ainsley?''

''I didn't mean to. I tried to finesse my way out of the question, but Scott wouldn't let it go. He wanted to tell everyone I was responsible for matching him up with Molly…as if I'd want people to know I'd put together such a mismatch. I reminded him that he'd promised to keep my secret. That he'd sworn he'd never reveal my part in the setup, not even to the woman I'd matched him with. But at the rehearsal, he was like a little kid, so excited and emotional and wanting everyone to understand how happy he was. There was a lot of champagne flowing, which didn't help matters, and suddenly, he stood up and told the entire gathering he and Molly owed their happiness all to me and that they were going to name their first child after me.

"Needless to say, it was an awkward moment and before I realized how it would sound, I blurted out that if I'd had anything to do with it, he'd be marrying Shelby Stewart, not Molly." Ainsley winced at the memory. "The minute I saw the look on Molly's face, I knew she realized I'd never intended for her to meet Scott, that I'd meant him to meet Shelby instead, no matter what he believed."

"Scott told her you'd set up that initial meeting at the restaurant?"

"Probably the first words out of his mouth." Ainsley shifted in the chair. "He's even worse at discretion than I am."

"Perhaps it would have been better if you'd kept your own counsel," Ilsa said, her smile unexpectedly gentle. "But Ainsley, I don't see how you can take the blame for everything that happened. Your only true mistake was in concluding the outcome of your *introduction of possibilities* was the wrong one."

"Please don't try to make me feel better, Ilsa. Scott and Molly aren't simply a bad match. They're totally wrong for each other."

"You seem so certain about that."

"If you spent five minutes with my cousin, you'd be certain, too."

Ilsa considered that, as she checked her watch.

"You'll discover, Ainsley, if you continue your apprenticeship, that an *introduction of possibilities* is fraught with...well, with possibilities."

"Is one of those possibilities my unemployment?"

"What?"

"Are you going to fire me?"

"Of course not."

"But I did the very thing you asked me not to do, the one thing you cautioned me about."

"You're guilty of trying to predict the future, Ainsley. That's hardly the crime you're trying to make it out to be. We all do it from time to time. Unsuccessfully, for the most part."

"You wouldn't have made this kind of mistake. You know you wouldn't have."

"I've made my share of mistakes, Ainsley. I still make them. Look at Peter and Thea Braddock. I was certain my intuition was leading me astray with them. While it worked out to be a true love match in the end, I'm still convinced that my part in it was misguided at best."

"They're perfect together." Ainsley couldn't believe Ilsa had any lingering doubts about the match. "Besides, I felt the same connection between them that you did. I encouraged you to put them together and, as they say, 'all's well that ends well.'"

"We did close the Braddock files rather successfully, didn't we?" Ilsa's slow smile hinted at the depth of her own successful romance with James

Braddock, the father of Peter, Bryce and Adam. Ilsa had made matches for all three of James's sons the previous year. Now she was rediscovering a happiness she hadn't known was possible. Ilsa hadn't married James as yet, but Ainsley thought it wouldn't be long. And Ainsley herself deserved some credit for that romance, since she'd personally encouraged, prodded and pressed Ilsa to give James a chance.

"Maybe you would have set up the possibilities differently for Thea and Peter if you had it to do over again," Ainsley said. "But the result is still a love match. Thea and Peter will only be happier together as time goes on. That wouldn't have happened for Scott and Molly. They're too much alike."

"Many wonderful marriages are built on similarities and shared interests, Ainsley. Having a great deal in common is usually an asset in a relationship. Look at your parents. They're a perfect example."

Ainsley's parents were the perfect example of having so much in common there wasn't room for anything else, but of course, she couldn't say that. Not to Ilsa. Not to anyone. "If Mom and Dad weren't so totally dedicated to their work for The Danville Foundation, I'm not sure they'd have anything at all to talk about."

Ilsa laughed. "Four wonderful children might warrant an occasional conversation."

Ainsley wasn't sure her parents realized they *had* children. They'd been gone nine or ten months out of every twelve for as long as she could remember. There could be no argument that The Danville Foundation dealt in noble causes or that its work was necessary and courageous. No one would ever accuse Charles and Linney Danville of being selfish, or of putting anything—not even their own family—above their commitment to their calling. For all practical purposes, their life's work had required that Matt, Miranda, Andrew and Ainsley be orphans so that less fortunate children in other parts of the world could be saved from hunger, disease and disasters.

But as she'd always done, Ainsley shook off the feeling she'd been cheated somehow in the parenting sweepstakes. It was an unworthy thought and made her feel heartily ashamed of herself every time it bobbed to the surface. She returned her attention to Ilsa. "If my parents ever had a difference of opinion about anything, it probably would make headline news around the world. They even finish each other's sentences."

"You say that as if it's a bad thing. I imagine Charles and Linney have had to depend on each other much more than most couples because of the nature of their work and the dangerous situations they're often faced with. For them, having that innate understanding of each other could very well be a matter of survival."

"I didn't mean it in a negative way," Ainsley said, hastily covering her tracks. "I'm just saying that if one of my parents had come to you as a client, you'd never have put them together as a couple.'' She didn't believe her parents would have married in the first place, much less stayed married for thirty-five years, if not for their absorption in, and dedication to, their humanitarian work. But she'd only voiced that opinion once, a long time ago, when she'd announced to her siblings her belief that Charles and Linney did not belong together. To say Matt and Miranda had given her a serious scold was putting it mildly. ''You'd have chosen someone very different for both of them. You know you would have, Ilsa. I know you would have.''

''Perhaps,'' Ilsa said with a smile. ''Which doesn't mean I'd have been right. The business of making matches is nothing if not subjective, Ainsley. I bring my own prejudices into it, just as you will. Despite your intentions for him, Scott fell in love with Molly. And even if, as you claim, they are too much alike to ever find a true happiness, that's their discovery to make. You need to remember that we, as matchmakers, are merely facilitators of romance, not the judge and jury of whether or not the match will be successful. Once you've set the possibilities in motion, your role is to step back and observe what happens.''

Ainsley smiled for perhaps the first time since the wedding. Or rather, the non-wedding. ''So do you think I should set up another *introduction of possi-*

bilities and hope that this time Scott will sit down at the right table and fall in love with Shelby?''

"Absolutely not," Ilsa said firmly. "Let your cousin work this out for himself. He will, believe me. Fortunately, as it happens, I have plenty of research to keep you busy while I'm away.''

"You're going away?"

Ilsa's smile held intimations of a sweet secret as she picked up a stack of files from the corner of her desk and offered them to Ainsley. "For two whole weeks. Maybe longer.''

"You're going away?" Ainsley repeated as she took the files, the sheer weight of them telling her she could be busy putting together the necessary information for a very long time. She could hardly pretend she didn't get the message. "By yourself?"

"James and I are taking a Mediterranean cruise. He's managed to schedule some time off between training his replacement in Colorado and taking up his new position with Braddock Properties, so we're stealing away for some R&R.''

"Wow," Ainsley said, her spirits rebounding with their normal enthusiasm. "I'm impressed. Any chance you'll put the man out of his misery and marry him before you return?"

Ilsa's smile deepened. "You never know what might happen," she said, then relented. "We're having a small, family wedding before we leave.''

"Then what are you still doing here? Go home and plan a wedding."

"What a lovely thought," Ilsa said warmly. "I believe I'll do just that." She slipped the strap of her bag over her shoulder and came around the desk. "We're leaving Friday, so you can reach me at home until then. After that, I'll call you every few days just to make sure you haven't run into any problems."

"Don't worry about me," Ainsley said as they walked out together, the idea of being in charge at IF Enterprises for almost three weeks percolating with possibilities. "I can manage the office, and with all this research to do—" she indicated the file folders in her arms with a lilting shrug "—you know I'll be too busy to even think about doing any more matchmaking on my own."

"I'm counting on that," Ilsa said, walking purposefully in the direction of the lobby.

Ainsley turned toward her own office, promising herself—and Ilsa in absentia—that she would stick to that resolve, no matter what.

Pushing the door inward with a bump of her hip, she paused for a second to appreciate the exquisite thrill she felt every time she entered this room. Her own office. And it had a view. Not so magnificent as the view of Newport Harbor that Matt saw every day through the windows of his office. Nor as pristine and pretty as Miranda's view of the botanical garden which bordered her office, also in the Danville Foundation building, which provided untold inspiration for the landscapes and interiors she designed with such a detailed eye for color and space. Certainly not the sort of view Andrew claimed, even though he had little use for an office at all. His photography kept him outdoors or in his studio darkroom, and even Ainsley would have been hard pressed to say which he preferred.

Despite the fact that her view was blocked by another office building and showed only a sliver of sky, Ainsley had no desire to change a single thing about her office. She loved it, wall to wall, ceiling to floor, furniture, accessories, everything. She loved being able to say, ''I'll be in my office.'' She liked knowing there was a place for her to go, work for her to do, somewhere she was needed and appreciated.

She liked being taken seriously, too…even if her first matchmaking attempt hadn't done much to project that image. Ilsa didn't seem to feel she'd permanently damaged her potential, though, so she was still on track to prove herself to her siblings. She would show them she was as serious about her career as they were about theirs. She wanted them to see her as an equal, an adult, and more than just their baby sister. As often as not, they still called her Baby, a nickname she disliked, but one that they considered affectionate and cute, despite her numerous complaints on the subject.

She'd win their respect yet, and make them proud of her...or die trying. She would.

For the time being, however, she'd concentrate on the research, just as Ilsa had asked her to do.

Ainsley's phone buzzed and she hurried toward the desk so she could answer it. "Yes, Luce?" she said into the speaker.

"You have a guest."

A guest. A *client,* maybe. Excitement bubbled up inside her. "Be right out!"

Dropping the files onto her desk, Ainsley headed for the reception area and her guest, hoping it wouldn't turn out to be Bucky. The last time he'd dropped by her office, he'd sweet-talked her into taking the rest of the day off to help him shop for his mother's birthday gift. As if she could just come and go as she pleased. As if her job wasn't that important. As if he wouldn't just buy a Hermes scarf for his mother's birthday as he'd done every year for the past four years he and Ainsley had been dating.

It was true that Bucky wasn't particularly original in his gift selections, although no one could fault his thoughtfulness in remembering special dates. Even occasions that most men wouldn't consider worth remembering—like the four-month anniversary of their first dance or the two-year anniversary of their first kiss—were marked in his PalmPilot.

That was one of the things she liked about Bucky. He was steady, cautious and organized—three qualities she sometimes wished she had herself. She and Bucky had things in common, of course, but it was their opposite traits, the contrasts in their personalities, that made them a good match. Maybe a lifetime match. Ainsley hadn't exactly decided about that possibility yet.

But the man standing by the front desk chatting amiably with Lucinda wasn't Buckingham Ellis Winston, IV.

And the thrill that went through Ainsley at the sight of him was nothing like what she felt for Bucky...or anyone else.

"Ivan!"

He turned in time to see her fly across the lobby, smiling her delight as she launched herself into his arms. "What are you doing here? When did you get into town? Why didn't you let us know you were coming?"

Ivan laughed as the words poured out of her in a rush and she wrapped him in a warm and enthusiastic hug. The first time he'd met Ainsley, she'd been a cute little thing on the verge of gawky adolescence, with a handful of freckles across her nose, a mouthful of braces on her teeth and some remarkably big ideas. He'd been twenty, determined, driven and very much aware of the difference between his background and that of the Danville clan.

Unlike Matt Danville, his college roommate, who'd been destined for the Ivy League since birth, Ivan had gotten into Harvard on a wing and a prayer. And it took every dollar he could scrape together to stay there. His parents couldn't help much at all because his younger sister's illness had wiped out what little they'd ever managed to save. Emma had died several years ago, just shy of her twelfth birthday, but the accumulated bills still had to be paid, so Ivan applied for a combination of scholarships, grants, loans and work-study assistance, and received enough to make Harvard possible. But there wasn't any extra money for trips home to Texas during school holidays, and even less for weekend entertainment. Ivan knew it was a fluke that he and Matt had wound up as roommates, but they'd quickly become the best of friends, providing opportunities for which Ivan would be forever grateful. Matt had invited Ivan to join him for weekends at Danfair, the Danville's ancestral home. He'd been included in trips to their beach house on Cape Cod and treated like a member of the family on many holidays and special occasions when Matt's parents, Charles and Linney, were home for a visit. And that was only the beginning of the opportunities he'd been given freely because of his friendship with Matt. Not the least of which was the opportunity to be Ainsley's *extra* brother, as she had dubbed him from the start.

"I just happened to be in the neighborhood," he said, his voice falling into the old teasing patterns he'd always used with her. "Matt told me you've started a new career, so I had to come and see what you're up to this time.''

She drew back, her hands still clasped loosely, affectionately, on his forearms. ''Matt knew you were coming to Providence and he didn't tell me?''

Ivan laughed. ''I guess that means he didn't tell you I'm going to be working just down the road from you, either.''

''You're kidding! You got a position with the Providence hospital?''

''Better than that.'' Ivan couldn't keep the pride from his voice. In all his dreams of making a difference in the world, he'd never thought he'd be granted such an opportunity so soon. ''Matt's asked me to head up the new pediatric research center for The Danville Foundation. I'll oversee treatment for the children with serious illnesses and work closely with the research team to develop the best regimen of therapy and medications for each patient.''

A flicker of dismay dimmed her smile for a moment, but it was so quickly gone he decided he must have imagined it. Ainsley was happy for him. She was always happy about everything. ''That's great,'' she said, and although he might have wished for a bit more enthusiasm in her voice, her dimples showed and her blue eyes shone with excitement. ''We have to celebrate! You have to come to Danfair tonight for dinner. And don't even think of saying no.''

Ivan didn't have the heart to tell her Matt had already extended a similar invitation. "You know I never pass up an offer of a free meal."

She tilted her head, giving him a sassy smile. "Oh, it's not free," she said. "It's going to cost you lots and lots of information. You have to tell everything you've been doing and the *real* reason you haven't been back to Rhode Island in five whole years."

"That'll be a short conversation. I've been in Phoenix, doing my internship and residency. In all that time, I've had less than three weeks off, none of it longer than thirty-six hours at once. *That's* the story."

"Do not think for half a second I'll let you off with that. No one works so hard they can't find a single second to make a phone call or send a postcard. Give it up, Donovan. I have a sixth sense for these things, and I'm sensing a demanding woman and a lurid romance tucked away in those years somewhere." She frowned suddenly. "You didn't get married and forget to tell me, did you?"

"Oh, no, ma'am," he said in his best and most exaggerated Texas drawl. "I've had no time for romance…lurid or otherwise. Being a doctor takes a big lot of energy and you know I'm nothing if not totally focused on my work."

"Your best and most exasperating quality," she said fondly.

The receptionist cleared her throat. Loudly. She was obviously anxious to be introduced.

"Lucinda." Ainsley obliged. "I'd like you to meet

Ivan. Dr. Donovan, this is our receptionist and all-around right-hand, Lucinda Reilly.''

He offered a handshake. ''I'm happy to meet you, Lucinda.''

''Likewise, I'm sure,'' she replied, darting glances at Ainsley as she let her hand linger in his. ''You should probably know I'm highly susceptible to cowboys and doctors.''

Ivan hadn't had a serious relationship for a long time, but he recognized an overture when it shook his hand. ''If only I'd brought my lasso or my stethoscope,'' he said.

''Don't be fooled, Luce.'' Ainsley took Ivan's arm. ''He's no match for you when it comes to flirtation.'' She looked up at him, raising her eyebrows in mock warning. ''Stay away from her, Ivan. She's the kind of woman your mother warned you about.''

''Hey, no fair,'' Lucinda protested good-naturedly. ''I didn't even get to ask him if he likes to dance.'' Her saucy *I'm available* smile winged his way once again. ''I'm a sucker for any guy who knows his way around a dance floor, too.''

''Or any other kind of floor,'' Ainsley said. ''Don't trust her, Ivan. She'll only break your heart.''

Ivan grinned, liking Lucinda's naughty-but-nice routine and loving the suggestion that Ainsley—even in jest—thought he needed to be protected from her. ''I'm the original klutz on the dance floor,'' he said with an air of regret. "Never even learned how to hokeypokey."

Ainsley pointed a silencing finger at the receptionist. "Do not even *think* what you're thinking," she said. "And he is much too innocent to hear it said aloud."

Lucinda laughed. "He doesn't look innocent," she said, reverting to a precisely professional voice as the phone rang.

"Oh, but he is." Ainsley tugged on his arm. "Come on. I want to show you my office. Can you believe it? I have an office!"

"So your brother mentioned." Ivan winked at Lucinda as he happily allowed Ainsley to lead him away. Busy on the telephone, the receptionist still managed to reply with a saucy wave of her fingers.

"And it has a view."

"Matt also mentioned the particularly stunning view."

She wrinkled her nose at him. "Oh, what does Matt know? He thinks I'm still six years old and playing Barbie Goes to the Office."

He'd almost forgotten how cute she was. Even at thirteen, with braces on her teeth and a body that was gangly and awkward, Ainsley had been captivating. Silver-blond curls, blue eyes, dimples and an infectious giggle put her firmly in the adorable little sister category. Ivan had never known exactly why she'd so readily adopted him as a beloved older brother.

Maybe it had been because Andrew often went traveling with their parents that year, while she'd been left behind to "improve her studies." Or because Matt had gone to college and wasn't there every day to fill the role of big brother. Or because Miranda was absorbed in her last year of high school and was impatient with the burden of being both mother and sister to them all. Probably it had been all of those reasons put together, plus more.

Whatever the reason, Ainsley had told Ivan—after he'd visited Danfair only a few times—that he would be her extra brother, and that's the way she'd treated him ever since. It was a role he'd accepted with particular delight, teasing her as he would have teased his own kid sister, Emma, had she lived to be thirteen.

"You look very…professional," he said to Ainsley, realizing that she did look quite grown-up in her azure blue suit, filling it out in a way he did not want to notice. He suddenly caught himself assessing the length of her skirt with a critical eye and checking the deep V of her blouse. She was showing a bit too much skin in both directions, but—extra brother or not—he knew better than to point it out. "This is a different, uh, style for you, isn't it?"

"I didn't think knickers and *Little Mermaid* T-shirts were quite right for meeting with clients." Her dimples made another appearance. "I know it's difficult for you and Matt to believe, but I'm not a little girl anymore." She stepped inside a large, lovely room and flung out an arm to encompass it all. "This is it. My office."

He took his time, walked about, looked carefully at the little touches that made this space distinctively hers. The photographs—all shapes, all sizes, all in heavy silver frames. The candles, scenting the room while casting a warm glow over the expensive furnishings. The not-quite-neat stacks of files on her desk. The colors—sunny, bright and cheerful. All of it reflected the exuberance of Ainsley. And yet, it was definitely a woman's space, and not what he'd expected at all.

"I like your office," Ivan said. "What do you do here?"

"Matt didn't tell you?"

"He said I should ask you. So I'm asking. What do you do here at IF Enterprises?"

"Me, personally, you mean?" She was stalling, something he'd seen her do only when she was nervous and wanted to say one thing, but thought it more prudent to say something else.

"Yes," he answered with a smile. "You, personally."

"Personal relations," she answered in a sudden rush. "It's like public relations, only on a more, uh, personal level. It's kind of hard to explain, but we do a lot of networking for people."

The only occupation that came to Ivan's mind involved résumés and high-level employment opportunities. "So IF Enterprises is some kind of elite employment agency?" he asked. "Matching a prospective client with the perfect position?"

"Something very much like that." She gestured toward the window. "Notice the view? It's really spectacular at this time of day."

It was a vista of solid brick, with a sliver of sky thrown in for effect. "Spectacular," he agreed. "I knew Matt was jealous the minute he mentioned it."

"My poor brother," she said with a husky giggle. "He doesn't even try to hide his envy anymore."

Ivan turned from the window and leaned back against it, feeling at home in a way he hadn't since he'd left New England for the southwest. "What do you have to do to get a view like this?" His glance strayed to the haphazard piles of manila folders on her desk. "Whatever it is, it must involve a lot of filing."

"Actually, Lucinda does the filing. My job, at the moment, is mostly research. I'm Mrs. Fairchild's apprentice."

"Apprentice?"

"More of an assistant right now," she explained. "But once I've learned the techniques, I'll be taking clients, too."

Clearly, she was proud of herself for landing this position, for having this office, the stick-your-head-out-the-window-and-look-up view of the sky. And he couldn't help but be proud of her, too, because she was so pleased with herself. He remembered all the times she'd confided her plans, wanting—needing—someone to listen and take her aspirations seriously. Matt, Miranda, even Andrew, had never seemed able to do that, so Ivan had been happy to be the "big brother" who listened and encouraged her to be whatever she wanted to be. He supposed, in their odd little family, her real siblings needed Ainsley to stay the baby, because it was important for them to feel they could protect her from the responsibilities they'd taken on too young. And as grown-up as she looked right now, there was still an air of innocence about her, a pure pleasure in her accomplishments. It was at moments like this that she reminded him of his sister, except that life had always sparkled in Ainsley, whereas in Emma it had never quite taken hold. "I'm happy for you," he said, approval in his voice.

"Thanks," she said, pleased. "I knew I could count on you to understand. Matt and Miranda—even Andrew, sometimes—think this is just another phase I'm going through and that I'll change my mind about making it a career. But I really love working here and, Ivan, I'm good at it, too."

"I never doubted it for a moment."

She smiled as she leaned against the desk and crossed her arms at her waist, her legs at the ankles.

She'd always been a petite little thing, but there was a serious amount of leg showing between the hem of her rather short skirt and her trendy little shoes. Ivan had never before noticed the length of her legs, or the lovely shape of them. He'd never realized she was so...curvy, either. It had been several years since he'd seen her, true, but she shouldn't have changed this much. Ainsley had grown up. Funny that he was so suddenly struck by that obvious fact. He'd have to get used to the idea that Baby had blossomed. Somehow just the thought made him uncomfortable.

"Matt said your folks are in Chile now."

She nodded. "They were supposed to come home for the wedding, but there was an earthquake and they needed to stay on."

"Wedding?" He didn't understand the swift clutch of emotion in his stomach. Surely if she'd gotten married, someone would have told him. "Whose wedding?" he asked casually. "Anyone I know?"

"Our cousin, Scott. Uncle Edward's son," she said...and Ivan was immediately, inexplicably relieved. "I don't know if you've met him or not. He's something of a loner." The corners of her mouth dipped into a rueful frown. "He still is, I guess, since the bride took off before the wedding and hasn't been heard from since."

"Wow. That must be hard for the family. Especially you."

Her head came up and a startled look flashed in her eyes. "Me? Why especially me?"

"Because you're so empathetic, always concerned

about other people and their problems, always wanting to fix whatever's wrong.''

"Oh," she said, relaxing. "You and I have that in common, don't we, Ivan?"

"We have a lot of things in common, Ainsley. Not least among them our passion for Ping-Pong. I do plan to beat your socks off tonight both before and after dinner. I've been practicing."

"So have I." She accepted his teasing challenge with a little toss of her curls. "And I was better than you to begin with. However, since it's your first time at Danfair in *five whole years,* I'll consider taking it easy on you."

"Oh!" He put a hand to his heart as if wounded. "Now there's a double-dog dare if I ever heard one. Don't even be thinking you'll *let* me win. I'll whip you fair and square, young lady, and don't you forget it."

She laughed, a pure and wonderful sound that made him feel warm all through. "I was merely thinking I'd give you a fighting chance, but if you're determined to be soundly defeated, far be it from me to deny you the humiliation."

He laughed, too, so glad to be in a place that felt so much like home, with someone who welcomed him with such open arms. "I'll look forward to our match, Ainsley."

"Me, too."

She had a smile worth the trip from Arizona, and he hoped she never stopped smiling at him.

"Guess I'd better leave you to your research," he said, moving to the doorway. "I sure don't want to be blamed if you don't get all your work done."

"How considerate you are, Doctor D." She tried to match his drawl as they walked together back out to the reception area. "But I happen to know you're heading for the nearest Ping-Pong pool hall to get in some remedial work on your backhand before tonight's match."

"That's where I'd rather be going, but I have an appointment with a Realtor this afternoon. Have to find a place to hang my hat, you know."

"There's an apartment available in my building," Lucinda offered, overhearing Ivan's last words. "You'd love it. *I'd* love it."

"I'll keep that option in mind in case the house deal falls through."

"You're buying a house?" Ainsley asked, her teasing replaced by the pleasure showing in her eyes. "Are you sure you don't want to stay with us at Danfair? We do have several extra bedrooms, you know."

He had loved every minute he'd ever spent in the grand old mansion on the cliffs at Newport. But living there…? No. He didn't belong and, silly as it seemed, he still harbored the secret fear that one day the Danvilles would realize it, too. He supposed that was the real reason he hadn't kept in better touch with them.

He'd talked to Matt on his office phone, of course, but had valiantly…and sometimes painfully… refrained from calling the house or even sending a postcard. Remaining close friends with Matt was one thing, but he'd wanted to give Miranda, Andrew and Ainsley some distance, a chance to take a step back from the one-of-the-family relationship he'd enjoyed. He should have known Ainsley, at least, would never allow that to happen. "I'm thirty-four," he said. "I think it's time I became a homeowner and paid property taxes like everyone else."

"I know someone who owns a lawn service," Lucinda piped up. "I'll give you my number, in case you ever need one."

"Ignore her." Ainsley guided him past the desk to the frosted-glass doors where IF ENTERPRISES was spelled out in flowing black script across both panels. "She thrives on the least encouragement."

"I'll remember that." Ivan said goodbye to the receptionist with a wave and leaned down to kiss Ainsley on the cheek. Her skin was flawless and smooth to the touch. Her scent was fresh and inviting, appealing and sweetly sassy, and he suddenly felt uncomfortable being so close to her. But he'd often kissed her goodbye like this. She always greeted him with a hug. A sisterly hug. Just as this was a very brotherly kiss.

Except that he wasn't her brother.

Ivan pulled back and opened the door with a slight jerk. "See you tonight," he said.

"Tonight," she replied, watching him go from the office into the hallway, where he became just a tall, shadowy form on the other side of the glass and then disappeared completely from view.

"Wowza." Lucinda followed up with a long, low whistle. "If he's in line for an *introduction of possibilities,* I'm available."

Ainsley shook her head. "Not even if I was thinking about putting together a match while Ilsa's away, which I'm not. I learned my lesson with Scott."

"Too bad he can't dance," Lucinda said with a sigh. "Do you think I should lower my standards this one time?"

"No," Ainsley said rather sharply, then softened the effect with a smile. "You're way out of his league, anyway. He needs someone much less experienced and much more…steady."

Lucinda wasn't the least offended. She was a wild child and proud of it. At first, Ainsley had wondered why Ilsa had hired such a flamboyant personality as the receptionist, but now, of course, she understood. What Lucinda lacked in restraint, she more than made up for in loyalty and a positive attitude, not to mention her often insightful, offbeat perspective. And, for all her flirty ways, she was crazy in love with Gus, her partner on the dance floor and off.

"Well, if he needs steady, do your sister a favor

and hook him up with her. She needs a man worse than any woman I've ever seen. No offense.''

None taken, because Luce was absolutely right. No one needed a love interest more than Miranda. Bossy, my-way-or-no-way Miranda. Who'd sworn off dating because it was tedious. Who tried far too hard to run Ainsley's life. And Matt's. And Andrew's.

''Ivan would be perfect for her,'' Ainsley agreed, and then was immediately appalled that she'd said the words aloud. She was even more horrified to feel the kick of adrenaline that signaled the idea was already taking hold as a possibility.

It was just a good thing she'd promised Ilsa.

It was just a darn good thing.

Chapter Three

Ivan had heard all the stories about Danfair having been built on pirates' gold.

On his very first visit, back when he and Matt were Harvard undergrads, Ivan had heard about Black Dan, the ruthless pirate who'd robbed, pillaged and plundered his way into wealth and a vigorous stake in the New World. Matt had told the legend with great enthusiasm and an amused nonchalance, which Ivan had found as fascinating as the tale itself.

"Absolutely," Matt had replied when Ivan asked the obvious question. "I believe all Danvilles have a drop or two of pirate's blood still coursing in their veins. Why else would we exercise this collective compulsion to save the world if not because we're trying to atone for old Black Dan's sins?"

Most members of the Danville clan, however, discounted as ridiculous any suggestion that one of their ancestors could have been less than a sterling character. As proof, they pointed to the humanitarian aid provided throughout the world by The Danville Foundation; the philanthropic work of the Danvilles in the nearly four centuries since the family had first arrived on the shores of New England; the way generation after generation had worked to turn sand into gold, beachfront property into retail businesses, which grew into national chains, which bought more properties in a cycle of success that increased the fortunes of all the Danvilles. And, of course, provided The Danville Foundation with the funds to continually expand their mission of helping those unable to help themselves. That much good could not have descended from the bloodline of a greedy, grasping, seafaring thief. It simply couldn't have happened.

Ivan didn't have any pirates in his family tree, and he sure didn't have any relatives who could afford to be philanthropists in order to expiate some ancient crime. The Donovans had a hardscrabble history. The only beachfront property Ivan's great-grandparents had owned was the sand in their shoes. His grandparents had been able to afford a small house. And while his own parents were coming up in the world— they'd scraped together enough to buy five acres— they were still a world away from the level of financial security the Danvilles enjoyed. A donation of outgrown clothing to the Salvation Army or Goodwill was as close to altruism as the Donovans had ever come. They were good people, strong and resilient in the face of hardship and tragedy, but without the his-

tory and pedigree Matt took for granted. Ivan had
grown up in a little Texas town where no one had
much money and where few of the residents had the
resources to even imagine another way of life.

Ivan was one of the few. He had imagined a different life. Because of Emma. Because he'd had to
watch her die in the heat of a relentless summer, without any hope of making her well…or even comfortable. He'd sworn then that one day he'd have the
power to make a difference. As Emma's life had
ebbed away, Ivan had committed his life to saving
children like her. He'd planned and schemed and
worked his butt off to get into Harvard, believing the
opportunities to fulfill his commitment would somehow arise from there. But he'd never expected the
biggest opportunity of all would come through his
college roommate. Matt Danville was more than a
friend. He was as near to a brother as Ivan would
ever know.

And Danfair, sitting like a pearl in the midst of
spectacular old country gardens, with a breathtaking,
panoramic view of the Atlantic, was as close to par-
adise as Ivan ever expected to come. It was a magnificent house, an American castle, built for beauty
and maintained with loving care. The first time Ivan
saw the gleaming white structure, nestled in a field of
green, with the seamless blue-gray ocean as its back-
drop, he'd been awestruck, unable to imagine what it
must have been like to grow up in such a place.

Behind the classical Ionic columns and huge ornate doors, he'd expected to find a lifestyle straight out of *The Great Gatsby,* an elegance unmatched even in his imagination—great works of art and priceless antiques, a hushed sophistication in every voice, a solemn, dignified, otherworldly existence. He'd expected to feel uncomfortable and out of place.

Instead, he'd discovered the unexpected.

Adorning the splendid architecture, there was certainly plenty of art and the luxuries that indicated great wealth, but those material things were of secondary importance compared with the lives of the young people who lived there. A few steps into the East Salon—so-called by Matt and his siblings—Ivan found a storybook lifestyle designed to nurture the Danville clan. Much to his delight, there was a dartboard on the wall, a jukebox in one corner, and stacks of books, board games and puzzles everywhere. A Ping-Pong table had been set up on the right side of the room and an eclectic mix of cushiony furniture was grouped around a television set on the other.

In the main dining room, a massive, dark, rich wood table was covered with jigsaw puzzles, bright, stubby crayons, all kinds of art paper and an assortment of paints. An indoor croquet field snaked from the library, through a reception room, along a wide hallway, and out to the entryway, where it ended just shy of the sweeping marble staircase. There was a small trampoline, center-stage, in a room whose original purpose Ivan had never been able to divine, and a larger trampoline on the wide back terrace. There was a collection of topiary animals in the east garden, a soccer goal on the back lawn and a maze of greenery that stretched nearly to the cliffs on the west side of the property.

Ivan's first glimpse of the long gold-and-white ballroom at Danfair had coincided with his first glimpse of Ainsley. She and Andrew were roller-skating on the beautiful parquet floors, racing like Olympians between the matching marble and gilt fireplaces that anchored either end of the great room. Ainsley had crashed into him with the reckless energy of a child. Barely thirteen at the time, she'd been mostly elbows and knees and odd angles, with untamed white-gold curls and eyes like an angel. She'd all but knocked the breath out of him with the accidental thrust of her helmet, so intent had she been on beating her brother in the race.

"Oops, sorry," she'd said in response to Matt's reprimand. Then she skated off again, trying to catch Andrew, who was already halfway across the room. But she looked back over her shoulder once with a shy little smile that had captured Ivan's heart.

At that exact moment, he'd understood he was welcome inside this elegant home, that Ainsley would never judge him for all he didn't have, but only on his willingness to accept her and her siblings for who they were inside these walls.

In all the years since that first day at Danfair, nothing much had changed. They'd all grown into adulthood, but the house still remained a curious mix of sophistication and playfulness. And Ivan still felt at home there, facing Ainsley across the table tennis net and trying his darnedest not to lose their first Ping-Pong match in years by a really humiliating margin.

"I thought you said you'd been practicing," Ainsley said as she served the ball with expert precision.

He neatly slapped it back. "Don't try to break my concentration. I know all your little tricks."

Her lips curved in a smile as she hammered the ball across the net, where it clipped the table just inside the line before bouncing up and over his shoulder. "My point, I believe," she said smugly.

"Lucky shot," he replied, and tossed the ball to her.

She arched one eyebrow in Ivan's direction, then poised for another serve. "Ready?"

"Set."

"Go." Ainsley swung, and the game was on again…for about fifteen seconds. Until the ball took a wicked little spin to the right as Ivan went left.

"My point, again," she said sweetly. "And it's still my serve."

He retrieved the ball and handed it to her across the net. "I'm only letting you get a few points ahead before I move in for the kill."

"Mmm-hmm." She touched the tip of the paddle

to her chin and looked at the ceiling. "Let's see, now. Does that make the score four thousand, eight hundred and thirty-seven to two, or four thousand, eight hundred and thirty-seven to three?" Her smile was coy and enchanting. "I just want to be sure I didn't miss one of your points in there, somewhere."

"Very funny," he said in mock displeasure, wondering when she'd gotten so sassy.

"Thank you," she said sweetly. "I've been practicing."

"What? Beating the pants off your dinner guests?"

She served the ball. "Oh, well, if you want special treatment, Ivan, I suppose I could *let* you win."

He sent the ball back with a nasty backspin. "You've developed an attitude since I've been away, Ainsley. I'm surprised Miranda lets you get away with it."

Ainsley shrugged, dimples flashing, as she met his challenge and returned the ball in an easy backhand. "I've frustrated her efforts to reform me for so long, I think she's finally given up. You should be careful, though. She's always on the lookout for a new challenge and you could be it."

"Miranda's not going to waste her energy on me. Why, I'd take more polishing up than that shiny little Mercedes she drives."

"You don't think *she* has anything to do with the actual polishing, do you? Miranda commands and, voilà, shine happens." The ball moved in a fast, steady rhythm, back and forth across the net. "Which doesn't mean you should underestimate my sister's energy level. She's the quintessential expert when it comes to fixing someone else's problems."

"It's a good thing I don't have any problems that need fixin', then." Ivan had to lunge to return a hard shot, but he managed to get it back with some credibility.

Ainsley laughed as she easily bunted it back. "I may have phrased that wrong. I should have said Miranda's a ball of fire when it comes to fixing someone else. Problems are optional."

Ivan was pleased to see that Ainsley hadn't lost that cute bounciness he'd so admired in her as a child. From bouncy curls to the way she bounced on the balls of her feet, Ainsley still projected a mischievous innocence that was head-to-toe charming. At least it would be if she wasn't roundly sinking him in this Ping-Pong match. She'd gained an attractive self-confidence in the five years he'd been gone…and he liked that. He was happy to see her finally coming into her own after all the time she'd spent in the shadow of her very accomplished siblings. Maybe the new job with IF Enterprises had made the difference. Maybe it was the man in her life—Buckley, wasn't it?

The thought of a man in Ainsley's life bothered him—as it would any caring brother—and he missed the only easy shot she'd given him in the entire game.

"Ha!" Ainsley danced a jazzy pirouette at her end of the table. "My point—and that, Dr. Donovan, is the game."

He retrieved the ball and laid it beneath his paddle on the table. "I'd demand a rematch, but I'm afraid you'd accept."

"Don't tell me you let her beat you at Ping-Pong, Ivan." Andrew walked into the room and shrugged off a hefty backpack. He was a tall, good-looking young man with thick red hair, an easy manner, the Danville blue eyes and a smile as lively and welcoming as Ainsley's. "Now, we'll never hear the end of it."

"Do not listen to him, Ivan," she advised with a teasing twinkle in her eyes. "I'm better than he is, too."

Pretending to ignore his sister, Andrew began removing all manner of lenses and film rolls from the pockets of his vest and transferring them to the camera bag. "She knows no shame, Ivan," he said. "Lord knows, we've tried to teach her better manners, but she has this pathetic need to prove she's God's Ping-Pong gift to the world."

"You just can't admit I'm better at something." She tilted her head and gave Ivan a conspiratorial smile. "They're all jealous of me," she said. "Because I'm such a natural talent."

"It's true, Ivan," Andrew said as he patted his vest pockets in search of elusive film rolls. "She was born with a Ping-Pong ball in her mouth. We have the pictures of her chubby cheeks to prove it.''

Ainsley made a face and Ivan laughed.

''What's so funny?'' Miranda entered the room like a song, lovely from every angle.

''I just whipped the socks off of Ivan,'' Ainsley announced happily. ''I beat him by four million, three hundred thousand and twenty-two points.''

''It was a mere four thousand and something,'' Ivan corrected. ''If we go by your scorecard.''

''What are you saying, Doctor? That these cheeks—'' Ainsley pointed to her irrepressible dimples with expressive index fingers ''—would *lie?*''

Ivan couldn't help laughing. ''I beg your pardon. My mistake.'' He turned to Miranda. ''She beat me by four million, three hundred thousand and twenty points.''

''Twenty-two,'' Ainsley happily corrected.

''Well, that's certainly hilarious,'' Miranda said. She was blond, blue-eyed and beautiful, and carried herself with a stately grace. Her smile was breathtaking, but lacked the genuine enthusiasm Ainsley brought to every expression and occasion. In other words, Miranda had gotten all the elegance, while Ainsley had inherited the bounce.

Ivan had always thought Miranda exquisite, with the untouchable loveliness of a work of art. She was self-possessed and assured, strong and confident. As a matter of course, her way was the right way, but he'd also known her to be generous when—*if*—it turned out she'd been wrong. There had been a time when she was the woman of his dreams, although he'd never had the courage to openly pursue her. In his heart, he supposed he'd felt he could never be good enough for her, and he didn't want to risk straining his friendship with Matt.

Now, suddenly, Ivan understood that this decision had had little—if anything—to do with his respect for Matt's friendship or even his own middle-class background. It had been based on something much more fundamental. He wasn't attracted to Miranda. Not in the way a man would have to be to romance her. She was a high-maintenance female, the kind of woman who required a slow, persistent courtship. Ivan hadn't had the time then, and he didn't have the interest now.

It wasn't that he didn't like Miranda. He did. She was the glue that bonded this branch of the family together, the anchor that kept them from drifting into stormy seas. Whatever her dreams were now—or once had been—she'd surrendered them to a higher calling—the family. Ivan appreciated her sacrifice. He admired her management skills, her attention to detail, her willingness to be the one in charge. He enjoyed her company, her fascinating combination of brains and beauty. He considered her a friend, someone who liked him and would stand firmly in his corner in a crisis. But, with Miranda, he'd never felt the

intimate and unswerving acceptance Ainsley had be-
stowed on him from the start.

"Bucky just buzzed in from the front gate," Miranda announced. She leaned down to remove a scrap
of paper from the carpet, and when she straightened
up, the creases in her linen slacks fell magically, perfectly, into place again. "He'll be at the door in a few
minutes. You'll want to be there to greet him."

"He knows his way to the salon," Ainsley said.

"He's still a guest, Baby," Miranda reminded.
"*Your* guest."

"Oh, please." Ainsley rolled her eyes. "Bucky's
about as much of a guest as Ivan."

Ivan felt a surprising twinge of pique at being
lumped into the same category as the unknown
Bucky.

"He'll expect you to be there, nonetheless."

"I'm sure he'll recover from that terrible disappointment."

"Ainsley." Miranda pronounced her name with the
authority of a sibling who's had to stand in for a
parent enough times to be comfortable in the role, to
feel, in fact, that it is her obligation. "You're a Danville. You weren't raised to treat anyone with disre-
spect. Especially not the man you plan to marry."

Ivan's stomach tensed. Ainsley *engaged*? Why
hadn't Matt told him? He'd mentioned Bucky, but
had said not a word about him being her fiancé.
"Whoa. Back up," he said, breaking into the dispute.

"What's this? I didn't know you were making wedding plans, Ainsley."

"I'm not," she replied, frowning at Miranda.

"Yet." Miranda smiled knowingly at Ivan. "Bucky's a very nice young man. You'll like him, Ivan."

Ivan disliked him already…for no good reason. "If he's Ainsley's choice, I'm sure I will."

"We're only dating," Ainsley said, her tone tight and defensive.

Miranda's smile was patient. "I didn't say you were going to marry him tomorrow."

"I've never said I'm going to marry him at all." Ainsley lifted up her chin as she spoke, but Ivan heard the thread of doubt in her voice, the underlying belief instilled in her since childhood that Miranda was always, essentially and *finally* right.

"Then why are we talking about it now?" Miranda turned her attention to Andrew, who was still focused on arranging the items in his camera bag. "Drew, you really should be getting ready for dinner."

Ainsley rolled her eyes and wished Miranda didn't always have to be so bossy.

"On my way, sis," Andrew said, continuing to do exactly what he had been doing—and would continue to do—until he was through. He couldn't be hurried when it involved his camera equipment, and he seldom paid the slightest attention to his big sister's nagging anyway. Not that being politely ignored would stop her from trying. Miranda was nothing if not persistent.

"How about a friendly game of Ping-Pong, Randa?" Ainsley teased her sister with a look, then upped the ante. "I'll spot you a thousand points."

"I'm not playing table tennis with you," Miranda said evenly, moving to sit on the sofa. "You don't play by the rules."

"Yes, I do. I'll even let you keep score."

"No, thank you. Drew? Would you mind?"

Ainsley caught Andrew's eye and shrugged, resigned to the fact that she could not distract their sister from her purpose. She'd known, of course, that Miranda wouldn't play, no matter who kept score, or how carefully. Ping-Pong or pinochle, Miranda didn't play games anymore. Sometimes, it seemed as if her sister's strong sense of responsibility had leeched away her ability to have fun. She needed someone—a man—to teach her that life didn't have to be taken so seriously. To show her that relinquishing her need to control life's every little detail could be a good thing. She needed someone—a man—to help her understand there was more to life than keeping a tight rein on her every emotion. The truth was, Miranda needed to fall helplessly, hopelessly, in love.

And the perfect someone—Ivan—was standing right in front of her.

But did Miranda notice? Was she even aware of how gorgeous he was? Or how his eyes were such a warm, wonderful shade of brown? Did she appreciate his smile? His intelligence? His sense of humor? His love of life?

Oh, no. Miranda was too busy trying to move Andrew and his miscellaneous camera equipment out of the salon because clutter bothered her. She was too busy fretting over Ainsley's reluctance to greet Bucky at the door because Miranda thought it showed bad manners. She was undoubtedly anxious, too, because Matt was late getting home and dinner might have to be delayed. Miranda didn't need an excuse to be uptight, but that never stopped her from looking for one. Little wonder she'd recently sworn off dating. She used up all her energy worrying about unimportant details. She spent her time trying to control things that ultimately made no difference.

As a sister, Ainsley wanted to help. As a professional—albeit apprentice—matchmaker, she knew Miranda needed, desperately, to discover the beautiful chaos of falling in love. The right man would soften her compulsion to control all the little things in her siblings' lives while missing the bigger picture in her own. He would transform her, make her a new woman, ease the weight of too much self-inflicted responsibility. Ainsley knew it could happen, felt in her heart it *would* happen…if only she could get Miranda to take one good, long look at the perfect man.

At Ivan.

Which wasn't to say he was perfect in every way. Just perfect for her.

If only Miranda could see that….

If only Ainsley hadn't made a promise….

"Ivan?" Miranda, smiling, her posture model straight, her back perfectly parallel to the back of the sofa, called him to her side. "I wanted to congratulate you on your new position with the pediatric center. We're all very pleased you accepted."

"I'm thrilled to have been offered the opportunity. I still can't quite believe it Why, I've hardly been able to sleep at night for pinching myself." Ivan's voice betrayed his deep sense of accomplishment. He perched on the arm of the sofa beside her.

Miranda, being Miranda, casually shifted her torso just enough to avoid any possibility of physical contact. Not because she thought that Ivan would make any kind of overture, but because she unconsciously avoided touching anyone. She wasn't a touchy-feely kind of person.

Ainsley knew that if she'd been the one sitting next to Ivan, she'd want to be close enough to feel the accidental bump of his arm against her shoulder, to enjoy the occasional, companionable touch of his hand, to absorb the unexpected warmth, the fleeting sensation of skin skimming over hers. She loved the little "oops" expressions that so often accompanied the unintentional brush of bodies. She simply loved being close to another person and knowing, in the depths of her being, that she wasn't alone. Maybe that was part of being born a twin. Or maybe she would have been that way regardless.

But Miranda was different. Distant. Difficult to reach. And it was going to take more than a man—even the *right* man—sitting next to her on the sofa to introduce any possibilities to Miranda.

Ainsley frowned, reminding herself—again—that there wasn't going to be any *introduction of possibilities.* At least not for the next three weeks. She'd told Ilsa she could mind the business *and* stay out of trouble. Not one or the other. Both. Which meant no matchmaking.

No matter how tempting the prospect.

"We're all excited to have you working with us," Miranda was saying to Ivan. "Mom and Dad asked me to tell you how pleased they are, as well."

"Thank you, that means a lot to me."

The door chimes echoed faintly, and Ainsley felt the weight of expectations turn in her direction. Miranda didn't even glance at her, but nonetheless, Ainsley obediently headed toward the foyer to do what was expected of her.

Apparently, Andrew felt the same internal pressures because he'd gathered his things and was following her out.

"Having Ivan here again is great, huh," he said, slinging the bulky backpack up onto his shoulder as they walked. "Matt's always hoped he'd come to work for the Foundation one day."

"I'm glad he's back," she said honestly, but she couldn't help wondering how long it would be before the Foundation sucked Ivan into its vortex of selfless martyrdom. She was instantly ashamed of the thought, ashamed of thinking what his sacrifice might mean to her instead of the benefit he would bring to so many others.

The Danville Foundation was her parents' passion, their raison d'être, their heart and soul. Their humanitarian work was also exhausting and demanding…and more important to them than any other person or thing, more important even than their children. And there were moments when Ainsley resented that. She didn't think she could bear to see Ivan get swallowed up in the worthiness of the work, too. And yet she knew he'd lose all respect for her if he had even an inkling of how selfishly she wished that wouldn't happen.

She and Andrew reached the entrance hall just as Tomas—the latest in a steady stream of foreign-born household help brought to the States through the sponsorship of Charles and Linney—opened the door to admit Buckingham Ellis Winston, IV.

"Hello there, Andrew. Ainsley." Bucky handed off his soft-sided leather briefcase to Tomas. "Were you afraid I couldn't find my way to the East Salon?"

Ainsley smiled approval at Tomas, who was new

to his job, thanking him with genuine warmth, before she moved forward to greet Bucky. "Miranda thought you'd want a guide."

"And she thought I'd want to change before dinner," Andrew said. "So I'll see you later." With a fleeting wave of his hand, he took the stairs of the sweeping staircase two at a time and left Ainsley there with the man she supposed she'd marry one day out of habit.

Bucky had given her a rush the first semester of her second year at Brown, worn down her resistance to a relationship by the end of that year and been her steady beau ever since. He was four years her senior, handsome, sweetly attentive, had a serious eye for details and, on occasion, left her wondering if love was supposed to fccl so comfortable. But, on the whole, they were beautifully compatible, and their differences were complementary on practically every level. As Miranda liked to point out, Bucky provided a good balance for Ainsley's often impetuously high spirits.

He greeted her now as he usually did, with a brief kiss and a gentle pat on her shoulder. "Hello, Cuteness," he said. "How was your day?"

"Exciting," she said, easily inserting the sparkle she knew he expected to hear in her voice. "Ivan's here."

"The infamous extra brother? The paragon of fun

you've talked about incessantly since I first met you?''

''That would be Ivan,'' she said happily.

''Ivan, huh?'' He took her elbow and turned her back in the direction she'd come, his gesture feeling somehow more proper than impromptu. ''I'm looking forward to meeting him…finally.''

''Good, because I'm about to introduce you.''

But it was Miranda who did the honors, who stood there beside the sofa watching with a pleased smile as the two men shook hands, exchanged pleasantries. Ainsley watched, not entirely happy about the polite, assessing way they each sized up the other.

''You work with the Foundation, too?'' Ivan asked when that bit of information arose in the conversation. ''In what area?''

''I'm in finance. The allocation, bookkeeping and auditing arenas. I have my hands on just about every dollar that flows through the organization.'' He paused, gave a short laugh. ''Figuratively speaking, of course.''

''Sounds like a big job.''

Bucky's smile erred on the side of self-importance. On occasion, Ainsley felt he took a little too much pride in his position. It wasn't anything bad, really, probably nothing more than that age-old which-one-will-be-alpha-dog question men seemed to sometimes feel needed to be answered. But it bothered Ainsley tonight. Ivan was a member of the family. Not someone Bucky had to impress.

"I do have a lot of responsibility," Bucky said. "It's my job to ensure the work of The Danville Foundation is funded day after day, year after year."

"Well, it's good to know who holds the purse strings in any organization." Ivan smiled easily. "I may as well warn you now that you'll be seeing a lot of me. You'll probably get sick of seeing me, in fact, because I know the new pediatric center is going to need additional funding on a regular basis."

Bucky laughed. "The center is very well funded already...and it isn't even open to the public yet."

"The costs of research are constantly escalating and that doesn't even touch the rising operational needs involved in caring for children with life-threatening diseases."

Bucky's solid shoulders squared another half-inch. "I strive to be fair, Ivan, but you have to understand that no one area of the Foundation's work can have every dollar they ask for. We do have to live within our budget."

"Or get a bigger budget," Ivan said, winking at Ainsley.

"I should probably warn you—" Bucky continued "—that the family depends on my judgment, and my recommendations are given serious consideration by the board. It's my job to make sure we stay within our budget and, frankly, it doesn't matter one iota to me if you're on friendly terms with the director or not.''

Ivan shifted his stance, but maintained an easy, unthreatened smile. ''Matt is my best friend. His family is as important to me as my own. And I've never yet stepped on a friendship to get what I want.''

''Oh, I wasn't saying you'd take advantage. I just thought you ought to know where I stand right from the start.'' Bucky laughed, ready—eager even—to correct Ivan. ''I don't take advantage of my relationship with Ainsley, either. Just because we're engaged doesn't mean I expect, or receive, special consideration.''

''We're not engaged,'' Ainsley said, startled by Bucky's sudden claim.

''Engaged to be engaged,'' Bucky said, shrugging away her protest, keeping his focus on Ivan. ''When you're a little more knowledgeable about the many facets of the Foundation's work, Ivan, you'll understand why I'm sometimes forced to say no.'' He reached for Ainsley's hand in an obviously territorial move. ''Would you get me a cocktail, darling?'' he asked. ''I'm parched.''

''Of course.'' She withdrew her hand, wanting nothing more than to send him home without a cocktail or even a bite of dinner. She didn't know why she'd invited him in the first place. Tonight should have been just for family.

''Your *extra* brother seems like a nice enough fellow.'' Bucky followed her across the room, watched amiably as she mixed and poured him a drink. ''A little on the idealistic side, but I imagine he'll figure out the way things work pretty fast.''

''Yes,'' she said, not even trying to keep the testiness out of her voice. ''But then it is idealism that has formed the mission of the Foundation since its inception.''

Bucky's eyebrows went up. ''I wasn't criticizing him, Ainsley. You're a little touchy tonight, aren't you?''

''That could be because you just announced our engagement as if it was official. We're not engaged, Bucky. You haven't asked and I haven't answered. Let's leave it at that.''

''We've talked about getting married in a year or two,'' he argued reasonably. ''I don't see why we have to pretend otherwise just because you have some old-fashioned idea it's not right for you to marry before your older sister does.''

Ainsley sighed. She'd never said that…exactly. She'd just shaped Bucky's perspective slightly because she wasn't sure she *didn't* intend to marry him. In a few years. After she'd proven herself as a matchmaker. After she'd grown tired of being independent. When she was ready to settle down to being a wife. But at times he pushed too hard. So she'd implied, without actually saying it, that her family felt her sister should be the first to wed.

"If I had my way, Miranda would marry Ivan and he could be my brother for real," she said, absent-mindedly.

Bucky frowned at her over his cocktail. "You can't be serious. She's completely out of his league."

"I don't think so," Ainsley said in a frosty voice. "I think they're perfect for each other. How can you look at them and not see that?"

"Easy. He's not her type."

"Oh, pooh." Ainsley thought they looked perfect together. Two beautiful people. A matched set, standing side by side. Miranda was tall enough to look regal beside his large powerful build. Her cool, champagne coloring and blue, blue eyes looked natural and right next to his dark blond, brown-eyed warmth. They had complementary personalities. Ivan would add sparkle to her life. She would handle all the little details of what was about to become a very complicated life for him. Together, they'd strike the right balance for a happily ever after.

Ainsley knew all of this in her matchmaker's heart…and she couldn't do a single thing about it.

Not at the moment, anyway.

Not even if some matchmaking emergency arose. Not even if she thought three weeks was too long to wait.

In a month, the new pediatric center would open and Ivan would be caught up in the constant, demanding and heartrending work of the Foundation.

He'd have no time or inclination for romance then, much less any opportunity to discover his true soul mate. He'd have no energy left over to explore possibilities for his own life. Ainsley could see a time—not too far off—when The Danville Foundation would consume him, would become his whole life, his heart and soul…just as it was for her parents. She could too easily imagine him lost to her in all the ways that really counted.

And she was determined not to let that happen.

If that was selfish…well, so be it. She didn't want to stop him from doing what he'd always hoped and planned and dreamed of doing. That would destroy something fine and wonderful inside him. She didn't even want to keep him from working for The Danville Foundation, if that's what brought him peace.

She just wanted to keep him as he was now. Alive to the possibilities of his own life as well as intent on saving the lives of others.

Bucky finished his drink and set the empty glass on the bar. "If you think it's a match, then who am I to argue? After all, you're the matchmaker-in-training. I'm just a glorified bean counter."

Normally that would have been Ainsley's cue to assure him his job was important, necessary, meaningful, that his modesty was misplaced. But tonight she felt strongly that her own job was the important one. The future of two of the people she loved most in the world might very well be in her hands.

She had faithfully promised she wouldn't do anything even remotely resembling matchmaking until Ilsa had returned and could supervise and consult.

But that didn't mean she had to stand back, wringing her hands for the next three weeks, while the opportunity to introduce some special possibilities evaporated.

The art of matchmaking was the art of finding out everything possible about a client, studying the likes, the dislikes, the beliefs, the secrets, everything it was possible to discover, and then watching for the spark that signaled opportunity. In this instance, she already knew more about Ivan and her sister than she would ever need to know about a client before introducing the possibility of a match. But there was no rule that said she couldn't offer Ivan some subtle coaching on how best to court Miranda when the time came.

He didn't have to know what she was doing. In fact, it was probably best if he didn't.

"Ainsley?" Bucky's voice interrupted her planning. "Would you mind fixing me another drink?"

"Certainly," she said, reaching for the carafe of wine, her mind still very much occupied elsewhere.

He stayed her hand just in time. "I'm drinking martinis," he reminded her. "What's going on inside that pretty little head of yours? What can be distracting you from paying attention to the man you're going to marry...someday?"

She didn't rise to the bait, didn't want her thoughts

sidetracked by having to lodge another protest. "Work," she replied, as she prepared to mix up another batch of martinis. "I'm thinking about my work."

"That could be dangerous."

Just then, from the far side of the room, she heard Ivan laughing. His deep, true baritone warmed her, and her high spirits returned in a bubbly rush. "Not if I do it correctly," she said with a sassy smile.

Chapter Four

As Matt pulled into a parking space in front of the new pediatric center, Ivan's pulse raced faster with excitement. The building was broad, low and appealingly solid. It was red brick, a traditional three-story structure set back out of easy view from the highway and, at first glance, looked more like an old elementary school than a hospital. There were lots of windows across the sturdy front, which gave an open, inviting look to the whole building…a little like an upside-down and oblong smiley face. The Danville Foundation did nothing by halves, and Ivan knew that behind those walls lay every available modern medical advancement to ensure this facility was state of the art from the first moment the doors opened.

He was happy they'd kept the basic design simple and child-friendly. It was a small detail, perhaps, in the overall planning, but an important one for the children who would soon be patients here. Removing the mystery from medical treatment was always one of

Ivan's primary objectives. His patients were scared enough as it was without adding a dark, foreboding facility into the mix.

"This is great," he said as he and Matt stepped out of the car.

"Welcome to the Jonathan Danville Children's Research Center," Matt said. "Your new home away from home. At least it will be in a little over a month, when it opens."

Ivan took a deep breath and just stood still a moment, fighting a curious mix of elation and anticipation. "This is great," he repeated. "Great."

Matt laughed. "There's still a great deal to be done before the opening. As you can see, they've barely started on the landscaping. There'll be topiary all along the front walk and meditation gardens accessible from either side of the wings. We wanted the grounds to be sheltered, but welcoming enough that families will feel free to seek out a small space of privacy and peace when necessary. It's difficult to tell from this—" his hand gestured at the lawn that was still mainly construction site and dirt "—but Miranda did an outstanding job with the landscape design."

"She always does an outstanding job," Ivan agreed, still staring at the building itself as his throat tightened with pride and pure raw emotion. The center was such a massive, magnificent undertaking. It would have a positive impact on so many children, so many families. And he would be a part of that. He

could hardly believe it, still. If there had been a facility such as this available to Emma, it could have
made all the difference. Her life might not have been
saved, but she would have been spared some of the
suffering and indignity of her illness. At the very
least, a place like this could have soothed his parents'
grief and anxiety, lightened their load, and maybe—
just maybe—kept his family from crumbling into un-
recognizable pieces.

"This is great," he said again, then grinned at
Matt. "I guess it's fair to say I'm impressed."

"That was a foregone conclusion." Matt clapped
him on the shoulder. "Come on, let me take you on
the VIP tour."

They approached the building on a newly poured
sidewalk and Ivan took it all in, tried to see the wide
glass doors the way a child would, imagined how his
little patients would feel as they stepped or were
wheeled inside the bright, open lobby. The windows
were lightly tinted against glare, which gave the reception area a warm, sunny feel. The lobby was
painted a bright blend of colors, with seascape murals
on the main walls. Child-size chairs were nestled in
with, or very near, the larger adult sofas and chairs.
There were blocks and beads, books and puzzles set
up in centers along one wall and a magazine rack full
of pamphlets and books about dealing with serious
diseases, all written in an easy-to-understand format
for both children and adults. Across the long front of

the reception booth, built right into the desk itself, there was a large aquarium which, when filled, would calm and fascinate young and old alike.

Ivan knew the first impression of any child entering this facility would be largely positive, despite their apprehension. He vowed then and there that he would do everything in his power to make the rest of their experience here just as positive. At least, as positive as was possible under the circumstances. That was the goal. His particular mission. The reason he'd been born healthy, while his sister had not. "Who's the architect?" he asked.

"Peter Braddock. You may have met him…or his brothers, Adam and Bryce. Their family's been in Rhode Island practically as long as ours."

"I don't think I have," Ivan said, because, despite having spent a lot of time at Danfair during his college years, Ivan had never done much socializing with Matt's society friends.

"I'll introduce you at the Denim & Diamond fundraiser Saturday evening. I'm sure the Braddocks will be there. They're all good men and good friends. You'll like them and their wives." Matt nodded as some workmen came through a side door and went out the front. "Braddock Construction is the contractor on the building," he said. "The work is a little behind schedule because of all the rain we had back in December, but since the Braddocks donated much of their services, we're not complaining."

"From what you've shown me so far, the design is perfect," Ivan said with sincerity. "I doubt anyone could have come up with better, so I'll look forward to meeting Peter and thanking him."

"We all had our share of input, of course. You know how these things evolve...plenty of ideas bouncing about, but someone finally has to pull them into a workable plan."

Ivan didn't know how projects like this evolved. He'd never had the experience of building anything, not even a house, but he could imagine the thrill of following an idea from inception to structural reality. He wished he could have been included in that process this time, but respected Matt's desire to surprise him with a job offer. "Let me guess," he said. "The murals were Miranda's idea, the aquarium was Andrew's, and Ainsley's contribution was enthusiasm."

"Ainsley actually wanted forest scenes on the walls, with lots of friendly, furry little creatures peeking out from behind trees and bushes. She even thought the office staff should wear animal costumes one day a week, just for fun. Miranda vetoed that suggestion as impractical, and overruled the forest scheme so the walls would tie in with the aquarium. There was considerable discussion over the colors—whether to do primary colors or pastels—but Miranda won that one, too. She thought reds and oranges would be overstimulating for the children. So, not to be left out entirely, Ainsley insisted we build a puppet stage and a dress-up center for the children in the less critical care ward. She's also plotting behind Miranda's back to have dress-up days for the staff, so she can get those animal costumes in one way or another, but I'm going to leave that battle for you to referee.'' Matt shook his head. ''If my sisters ever have a real argument, I hope I'm out of the country. There's a good reason most of The Danville Foundation's projects are governed by committee or department and not left entirely up to the family to decide. But the center was too near and dear to all our hearts. We wanted to be very hands-on.''

''Well, it shows.'' Ivan followed Matt through a doorway behind the reception booth and into a long hall of basic office space. ''This must be the administrative wing.''

Matt nodded. ''I warn you, we didn't do much in the offices. We felt our resources were better utilized in the patient area. But if you think the staff should have something more cheerful than off-white walls and plain workstations, feel free to submit a limited redecorating budget.''

''Are you kidding?'' Ivan asked with a laugh. ''You know if it were up to me, no one would have an office at all. The staff would just have to be resourceful about finding a clear spot to work.''

''Which is the reason you're here, Ivan. I know— we all know—the patients are the most important part of this for you.''

Ivan stopped walking to look at his friend. "I won't let you down, Matt."

"I know that, too." Matt moved ahead to open a closed door. "But you may want to take a look at your office before you get overcome with gratitude. I wasn't kidding about it being just four square walls and a few pieces of utilitarian furniture."

Ivan glanced inside, interested only in knowing where to go to do the paperwork. Unfortunately, there was always paperwork. "This is perfect," he said.

"Considering you don't plan to spend any more time in here than absolutely necessary?" Matt laughed and closed the door. "And to think I could hardly get you out of the dorm when we were in college."

"I had to study." Ivan defended himself as he did anytime the subject came up. "And the best place to do that was in the room. The best place for me to invest my time here will be with the patients, their families and the medical staff."

"You are the most dedicated person I think I've ever met." Matt led the way to another door, one that opened onto a back stairway. He started up the steps to the second floor and Ivan stayed close behind him. "And, believe me, I know several."

"I'm the laziest son of a gun in the world next to your mom and dad," Ivan protested.

"Yes, well, you're a lot younger than they are, too. It's taken them years to perfect their devotion to the

Foundation. And, for the record, I advise you not to follow their example to the letter. They've missed out on a lot.''

Ivan knew that was true, but still admired their willingness to make the sacrifice. ''But they've helped so many in the process.''

''They are—'' Matt admitted ''—remarkable people.''

''You're no slouch, yourself.''

''I'm a crusader by birth, Ivan. Left to my own devices, I doubt I'd have had the initiative to accomplish even half of what you've already accomplished in your life.''

''Save the modesty for someone who doesn't know you as well as I do. You're the power behind the scenes of this operation, Matthew. This clinic wouldn't exist if not for your ability to pull all those bouncing ideas into a workable plan. I know that…and so do you.''

Matt paused at the landing. ''Anyone in my position could do the same,'' he said. ''But if I'd had to start where you did and pull myself out by sheer grit and determination…'' He shook his head as he opened the door onto the second floor. ''That's where you'll always have the jump on me, Ive. You've got grit.''

There would always be that element in their friendship, Ivan supposed. That mutual disagreement over who had made the best use of their circumstances.

He'd started with nothing except the will to save his sister. Matt had started with the will to carry on the work his forefathers had begun. By rights, their paths should never have crossed, but here they were. Two men from opposite ends of the social spectrum who had found they shared a common goal. Ivan had no doubt his friend would have accomplished great things, regardless of his beginnings. Ivan, on the other hand, would never have had these opportunities at all if not for Matt and his family.

"Your parents set a wonderful example, Matt. The world would be a poorer place without them. Without The Danville Foundation. I'm more than grateful for your faith in me, and I'll do everything in my power to make the center a success."

"Tell me that again after you've attended your first fund-raiser gala." Matt held open the stairwell door and they moved out into the second-floor hallway. "Which is this coming Saturday. Or did I already mention that? At any rate, I hope you brought your black tie."

As the door closed behind them with a metallic click, the feel of a hospital corridor surrounded Ivan. Now he was in familiar territory. "I'm not sure putting me in a tuxedo and taking me to the ball will be of any benefit to the Foundation. You know I'm mostly inept in social situations. Remember the time you tricked me into taking your date's roommate to the Kappa's Winter Ball? That was a disaster."

"Hello," Matt said to a couple of workmen who were touching up paint in the hallway. "It looks good, gentlemen."

"Thank you, Mr. Danville," one replied.

"We're gonna have this section all finished by Friday," said the other.

"Great. I'm counting on you," Matt said and kept walking as he continued his conversation with Ivan. "You've been using that Winter Ball excuse to get out of your social obligations for years. It's time to step up to the plate, my man, and let the ladies have a chance at you. You'll be the man of the hour, I guarantee."

"And how, exactly, will that help the pediatric center?"

"Think of it as, 'Dancing for Dollars.' Some of the biggest contributions to The Danville Foundation have come from women who appreciate my ability to tango."

Ivan winced. "Now I know we're in trouble. You know how uncoordinated I am on the dance floor."

Matt dismissed any concern with a wave of his hand. "Anyone can learn to dance. It's the charisma that can't be faked."

"Oh, so it's okay if I trip my partner just so long as I'm charming while I help her up off the floor?"

"It's all in the wrist, buddy," Matt agreed with a grin. "And the smile. Never forget the smile."

Ivan flipped on the lights in the waiting room area

and was pleased to see that here Ainsley's personality had won out. The murals were cartoon animals, not furry or familiar, but bright, cheerful, odd little creatures, painted with a gleeful hand and a certain irreverent flair. "I see Ainsley was in charge of decorating up here."

"Hard to miss her free-spirited approach, isn't it?" But Matt seemed to appreciate the result. "You know, if you're worried about not knowing how to dance, you could get Ainsley to teach you. She's been taking dance lessons of one sort or another her whole life. She started out wanting to be a prima ballerina, progressed through tap, interpretive dance and, at her eleventh birthday party, startled us all by declaring she'd decided to become an engineer. She's always had trouble with math so, luckily, that phase passed in favor of something else. I forget what. That's our Baby. Never short on big ideas. It's just lucky for the rest of us she never maintains interest long enough to carry them out."

Ivan moved forward to take a closer look at the mural. "Did she paint this herself?"

"Every last curious little creature. She wouldn't let any of us come near this area until she'd finished. You can see why."

Ivan smiled, imagining Ainsley in coveralls, paint splattered all through her hair, across her face, concentrating furiously on making these murals her contribution to the children. "The kids will love it," he said. "She did a great job." He turned, walked back to the doorway where Matt waited. "I stopped by her office Monday. She insisted on showing me the view from her window."

Matt laughed. "She's always tweaking me about that. As if she doesn't get enough attention already."

"Do you like the accountant?" he asked suddenly, bluntly. "The one who came to dinner the other night."

"Bucky?" Matt answered with a shrug. "He's a nice guy. Comes from a good Boston family. He seems steady enough for her and he does a good job for the Foundation. A thankless job at that. She could do worse."

She could do better, too, but it wasn't Ivan's place to comment on Ainsley's love interest. Although he wanted to. He really wanted to. "What exactly is IF Enterprises?" he asked instead. "When I asked her, she told me their business is some sort of personal relations, but I got the feeling there was more to it than that."

Matt's expression softened, turned almost sheepish. "I suppose there's no harm in telling you, since she doesn't seem to be keeping it a secret. IF Enterprises specializes in happily ever afters."

"They write fairy tales?"

"That's the way I look at it," Matt said. "But according to Baby, IF Enterprises is in the business of matchmaking."

"Making matches?"

"Matchmaking," Matt repeated. "The kind between a man and a woman. The kind that has matrimony as its objective."

"You're kidding, right?"

Matt shook his head as they walked past the vacant nurses' station, and the dress-up play center—another of Ainsley's inspirations—nestled in the room directly behind it. "As it turns out, Mrs. Fairchild has been operating as an exclusive matchmaker for the upper strata of New England society for a number of years. Apparently with quite a record of successes, too. Ainsley badgered the poor woman shamelessly until she agreed to take her on as an apprentice."

A matchmaker's apprentice. He'd never have guessed, but he could see how that would appeal to Ainsley. She'd told him—in one of her confiding moments—that when she was a little girl, she'd wanted to grow up to be a fairy godmother. He could see where matchmaker might be an extension of that long-ago fantasy. She'd be good at it, too, with her imagination and enthusiasm, her keen eye for personalities and her boundless energy for helping others. Yes, he could see that given half a chance, she'd be very good at drawing people together, at spotting the potential for a happily ever after. "I wouldn't have thought there'd be much call for matchmakers these days," he said. "I especially wouldn't have thought it would be…acceptable…here."

"To the silver spoon crowd, you mean? Six months ago, I'd have agreed with you. But Baby has been educating me on the subject and it turns out it's not any easier to meet the right person here than it is to stumble across her in one of your Texas dance halls. Not that you would know this, Mr. Socially Inept."

Matt always tweaked him on that, teased him about his belief that the differences in their backgrounds were vast and diametrically opposed. It didn't change Ivan's thinking, but he appreciated the attempt, just the same.

"Maybe I should get Ainsley to do some match-making for me," Ivan said as a joke. "She could use me as a practice case."

"Be careful there, my friend. She tried to set up a match for our cousin and he wound up getting left at the altar. Besides, you might want to practice being an eligible bachelor for a while. Take it from me, being the man of the hour has certain advantages."

"Still leery of marriage traps, Matt? Don't you want to find the right woman?" He paused to smile. "Or at least give Ainsley the opportunity to find her for you?"

Matt shuddered at the thought. "No, and no. I've got all the commitment I can handle just managing the Foundation. By the time I'm ready to think about marriage, I'm sure some other occupation will have snagged Baby's interest."

Ivan wished Matt had more faith in Ainsley. He

wished she wasn't always treated like the baby of the family and never allowed to really, honestly grow up. But he certainly wasn't going to criticize the way the Danville children interacted. They'd grown up in an odd sort of cocoon, depending on each other because their parents were so seldom there. Many times over, Ivan had been welcomed in to share their good times, but he'd never been included in their struggles. If, in fact, they had any. "I just hope she doesn't get married and start producing little accountants with Bucky's haircut."

Matt laughed. "That's a scary thought."

"Worse than scary." Ivan didn't think he could stand to see Ainsley choose that kind of staid and stifling partner. It made his heart hurt just to think about it.

They completed their tour of the second floor and went on to the third—the surgical and critical care unit. Professionally, Ivan was thrilled with the innovations there, but he knew this floor would be hushed and heavy with the weight of too many lives cut short. There were no murals here—this wasn't the place for anything except intensive care and the hope for a miracle cure. It made him glad the Danvilles were sensitive to that aspect of the medical treatment the center would be providing. But he wasn't sorry, for now, to leave the area and walk to the wing that contained the research labs.

Ivan could have spent the next month happily

camped out in that wing, but Matt was hungry and wanted to get some lunch. "I'll get you some information about the Denim & Diamonds gala," Matt said over a sandwich from the Newport Creamery. "Time, place, etc. Wear jeans with a tux jacket and shirt. You can wear your cowboy boots, if you want, but don't forget the black tie."

The crabmeat sandwich suddenly lost some of its flavor, and Ivan chased a bite of it with a swallow of Sam Adams. "You're sure you want me to go? I don't think I'll be much of an asset."

"Ivan, my man, you have some wake-up calls ahead. The name of the game around here is who you know…and who knows you. From now on, your dance card is going to stay pretty full. This Saturday you'll make polite conversation for the benefit of the American Cancer Society. In a couple of weeks, you'll be lifting your glass in support of the Providence Symphony Orchestra. But down the road, I guarantee at least one of those conversations or one of those toasts will result in a substantial gift to the Foundation and the pediatric center. That's how it works."

"Okay, then," Ivan said, giving in with good grace if not much confidence. "I'd better get signed up for those dance lessons."

Matt grinned. "It's not a death sentence. You might even enjoy yourself for a change. When, exactly, was the last time you held a beautiful woman in your arms?''

''As a matter of fact, it was just the other day,'' he said smugly, remembering the warmth, the scent, the sweet pleasure of holding and hugging Ainsley.

''It was?'' Matt was momentarily taken aback, but then he came around. ''Getting a welcome-home hug from my baby sister doesn't count.''

''The hell it doesn't.'' Ivan picked up his sandwich again. ''She's a beautiful woman.''

''Yes, but too close to a sister to count. I know you're dedicated to your profession, Ivan, and that's important. But you may want to think about having a personal life now, too. Eventually you're going to want to get married and have a family. This may be the right time to start looking.''

''I could say the same to you.''

''No, that's where we're different. I don't intend to have children, which isn't something women want to believe. They think you'll change your mind—or they'll change it for you. So I don't see myself getting married. That's just the way it has to be. Someone else's son can carry the family responsibility into the next generation.''

Ivan had heard Matt say that about kids before, but hadn't honestly believed he meant it. Who wouldn't want children? A family of his own? Ivan had always had the idea in the back of his mind. For later. After he'd finished medical school. After his residency. After he'd found the place in the world he was supposed to fill. And it was true, all of those "laters" were behind him now. For the most part, anyway. Maybe it was time to open his heart to the possibility of finding the woman who would share his life…and his purpose.

"Dance lessons and a wife," he said drily as he pretended to make a list on a paper napkin. "I am going to be busy."

Matt laughed. "Just watch out for the matchmaker's apprentice."

Ivan laughed, too, but the idea struck him that he could enlist Ainsley's help. Not because he wanted her to find him a wife, but because he wanted to support her choice of career, as frivolous as he had to admit it sounded. It seemed no one else in the family believed she could succeed. And really, what was the worst that could happen? It might even earn her a measure of new respect from her family. She needed that. She deserved it. Who knew? She might set him up with someone who could actually teach him how to dance. He might even learn the tango.

Stranger things had happened. Look at how far he'd come. Look at the opportunity he'd been given to make a real difference in the world.

Proof positive that miracles did occur…even to ordinary guys like him.

"LINE TWO IS FOR YOU," Lucinda announced when Ainsley picked up the phone in her office. "Your brother. The picture taker."

"Photographer, Luce," Ainsley corrected. "Andrew's a freelance photographer."

"Okay, whatever." And the intercom light blinked off.

Ainsley jabbed the flashing line two. "Andrew?"

"Hello, baby sister! You are going to be so glad I called you today." Andrew's voice came across the phone line sounding overly cheery and a little desperate. "What would you say if I told you I've decided to take you with me on an all-expense-paid trip to Salt Lake City?"

Ainsley giggled into the phone, instantly happy to hear from her twin, even when she suspected he had ulterior motives. "First, I'd remind you that I'm a working woman and can't be away from my office at this particular time. Ilsa has left me in charge while she's away on her honeymoon, you know." A lilting thrill came with the words, the idea that she was really and truly the matchmaker's apprentice. "And second, I'd ask why you need *me* to help you lug your camera equipment all over creation. Haven't you hired a new assistant yet?"

There was a crash of metal in the background, a shriek of dismay far down the phone line and a heavy sigh from Andrew. "Don't even tell me what you just did, Hayley," he called out. His hand over the receiver didn't come close to muffling his aggravation.

"I do not want to know. Hold on a second, Ainsley. I'm going into the darkroom."

She heard the door close, the click of the switch that turned on the outside light—a red warning to anyone in the studio not to open the darkroom door.

"As a matter of fact," he said a moment later. "I have hired someone. Hayley Sayers. You may see her name listed under homicide victims any day now."

"Murder seems a little drastic, Andrew. Maybe you could just fire her."

"And do exactly what she expects me to do? I don't think so."

Hmm, Ainsley thought. "If you're not going to fire her, then she can accompany you on that all-expense paid trip to Salt Lake. Toting around some of your equipment might be all the encouragement she needs to quit."

"I thought of that, but she's like a little mule, stubbornly refusing to admit she isn't capable of doing everything I ask."

Hmm and *double hmm.* "How long has she been working for you?"

"Four days," he said, as another, smaller clatter—muted by the confines of the darkroom enclosure—made its way from his Newport studio to her office in downtown Providence. "Four long days. I can't decide if I'm more afraid to take her with me on this Utah trip or to leave her behind, unsupervised."

"Why?"

"I don't know, exactly. She's a little strange, that's all."

"Strange how?"

"She squeaks, for one thing. Makes this little *eek!* sound when she's startled…which seems to be most of the time. And she's twitchy. You'd think I was trying to sneak up behind her to shout, 'boo!' the way she jumps every time she catches sight of me."

"You probably intimidate the life out of her, Andrew."

"I'd like to think I'm instilling a healthy respect for the art of photography and especially my photography equipment, but it's obvious that strategy isn't working."

"So, why can't you just fire her?"

"Her portfolio is amazing, Ains. A couple of her black-and-white prints are so good I wish I'd taken them myself. Most of her work is still uneven, immature, but she's genuinely talented. There's no question she's got more potential than all of my former assistants combined. Unfortunately, she also has less than half of their collective confidence. So, she can quit anytime she wants, but I'm not going to fire her."

Ainsley's intuition perked up. She sat straighter in her desk chair. Andrew had little patience for mentoring, but he was a fool for anyone with real talent. That spark of potential snared him every time. Ainsley could count on one hand the people whose raw talent had earned them the level of admiration and respect she heard now in her brother's voice. Hayley Sayers might drive him crazy with her squeaks and starts and clumsiness, but he wouldn't fire her. He'd push and prod and provoke her to develop that potential, no matter how much havoc she wrought in his studio. Or on him personally.

"So," Ainsley asked in a carefully casual tone. "What's she like?"

"I just told you. Mousey. Jumpy. Nervous. Intimidated. That about sums up my new assistant."

"Is she cute?"

"Now, how would I know that?"

"You could look at her."

"There's not much to see. She wears baggy jeans that flap around her ankles when she walks, baggy T-shirts that hang on her like old paper sacks, hi-top sneakers, and dreadlocks."

It wasn't an encouraging description. "Dreadlocks?"

"With beads. Lots of beads that click together like chattering teeth when she makes a move. No, I wouldn't say she's cute, and whatever romantic plot your devious little mind is hatching, you can forget about right now. She's not my type and I am not interested."

"You're interested in her talent."

"And in her showing up for work."

"Which, apparently, she's done for four whole

days. Be a hero, Drew. Take her to Utah. There could be possibilities you can't even imagine.''

"For what? Camera repairs?'' He paused to clear his throat. ''You know, Ainsley, ever since you took this position with Ilsa Fairchild, you spend a lot of time talking about possibilities and introductions and romance.''

"I've always talked that way,'' she said. ''You only notice it now because of my profession.''

"I notice it now because I have the feeling you've got Cupid out there flying around, looking for my perfect match.''

"And so what if I did? You're my twin brother. I love you. I want you to be happy.''

"I am matchless and ecstatically happy that way. Do me a favor. If you must pursue this matchmaking thing as a career, would you please confine your victims to someone who isn't related to you?''

That stung just a little. Andrew had always been supportive of anything she wanted to do—including her efforts to obtain this position with IF Enterprises—but there were times she could tell he thought matchmaking was just another whim, one more fanciful possibility in a long list of potential careers that ultimately turned out to be not quite right. But she would prove herself this time. To Matt. To Miranda. And to Andrew. ''Take Hayley with you,'' she advised, the matchmaker and the twin sister in perfect accord. "Give her a chance to prove how helpful she can be."

A buzzer went off with a shrill alert on his end of the line. It was a warning that was plenty loud even in Ainsley's office. She knew what it was immediately—the opening of the darkroom door while processing was going on inside. "Hayley!" Drew yelled, his mood scratchy with temper. "Didn't you see the light…?"

The line went dead then. He'd hung up to deal with his printing problems and his new assistant. His *talented* new assistant.

Interesting, the matchmaker's apprentice thought.

MIRANDA GLANCED at the clock on the wall of Ainsley's office, then tapped the platinum casing of the watch on her wrist—as if it wasn't one of the finest Swiss timekeeping pieces on the planet and might actually be losing minutes right and left. "Time to go," she said, rising. "I don't want to be late for my luncheon."

Ainsley smiled, sliding to her feet from her temporary perch on the corner of her desk. "No, it would be simply awful if you were late."

"Don't start on me today, Ainsley. It is not a flaw to be punctual and to want to arrive on time for an appointment."

"No, indeed, it is not," Ainsley agreed. "And since one can never predict the delays that await you on the walk between here and the restaurant, it's essential to allow a few extra minutes to get there.''

Miranda's lips formed a tight little line, somewhere between good humor and complete exasperation. An expression Ainsley was very accustomed to seeing. ''One of these days, I'm going to be late just so you and Andrew will stop teasing me about it.''

''Wow,'' Ainsley said, impressed by the offer. ''Can I have that in writing?''

''No.'' Miranda tucked the straps of her handbag precisely on the middle of her forearm and folded her arm—quite unconsciously—in against her body. She wasn't quite thirty yet and at times she behaved like a much older woman. ''I'm not about to give you something tangible to hold over my head…even if you are merely teasing.''

Ainsley stepped in close to her sister, slipping a hand through the crook of that inflexible arm, giving Miranda a little hug of affection. ''We only tease you because you make it so easy,'' she said. ''It would be good for you to be late once in a while. Andrew and I would love it.''

''Mmm-hmm. Well, I wouldn't love it and it isn't likely to happen. Especially not today.''

''Why not? You know Carolyn never gets anywhere on time. She's chronically time-challenged.''

''Which somehow justifies my being late for our lunch date? Honestly, Ainsley, sometimes you don't think things through.''

Which was a matter of opinion. Her own versus theirs. *Theirs* being every other member of her family. She pulled her hand free as they reached the lobby and walked over to take the pink message slip Lucinda was holding up. "Thanks for coming by," she said to Miranda. "I'm glad you had that little gap in your schedule."

"I should have called first, but since I was in the area, anyway, I just thought I'd take a chance you weren't busy." Miranda didn't come by often and never simply dropped in, as she'd done today. She said it was because she didn't want to intrude into Ainsley's work time, but in reality it was because she so seldom had an unexpected gap in her schedule. And if there was one thing Miranda couldn't handle, it was having unscheduled time on her hands.

"I'm really glad you came by," Ainsley said honestly. "And I'm sorry I can't have lunch with you."

"No, you're not." Miranda made the smallest grimace. "Carolyn is one of the most tedious women we know, and I wouldn't have lunch with her at all if she wasn't co-chairing this year's benefit."

"She's a heck of a fund-raiser. You have to hand her that."

"I'm well aware of all she does and that we're fortunate she and her husband moved to Providence last year. If only she didn't talk so much, or so slowly...or take so long to get to the point. Sometimes I want to reach over and jerk the words right off her tongue.'' Miranda crossed to the door. ''The things we do for the Foundation.''

Ainsley agreed, but not in the same way or for the same reasons. Miranda wanted to run the Foundation…and would have been good at it, too. Better, perhaps, even than Matt. But The Danville Foundation was older than them all and tradition decreed the oldest ''Jonathan'' should be the head of the family trust. Matt, being the first-born son of the first-born son and therefore awarded the family name of Jonathan, had been anointed in the cradle. Miranda, being the second born and a daughter, besides, was left out of consideration.

She worked for the Foundation, seemed content to manage the trust's various properties and her own landscape design company, the profits of which helped support the Foundation. Environment was Miranda's calling. She knew how to set the stage to get things done, and she followed through to make sure they were done correctly. It was a talent Ainsley admired and occasionally envied. But not today.

''Have a lovely time,'' Ainsley said.

''Sure thing,'' Miranda answered as she pulled open the frosted glass door and breezed out.

''Whew!'' Lucinda released the word on a breathy exhale. ''Is she always that intense or did I just forget to take my Prozac this morning?''

Ainsley laughed and glanced at the call message in her hands.

"Ainsley?" Miranda was back, holding the door open. "I meant to tell you. Uncle Edward called this morning. He wants you to do something about Scott."

"What does he want me to do?"

"I don't know. He just said he was tired of seeing his son moping around and someone had to do something."

Ainsley frowned. "I guess I could invite him to lunch one day this week. Or to dinner."

"Not dinner," Miranda said a little too quickly, indicating *she* wanted no part of this *doing something* with Scott. Her fingertips tapped the leather clasp of her handbag. "Oh, I don't care. Bring him to dinner if you think that's best. I suppose as long as you don't try to set him up with another blind date, any distraction will do."

"It wasn't a blind date." Ainsley knew her sister— and her brothers, for that matter—didn't take her career seriously. Not a big surprise since they didn't take *her* seriously, much less her choices. In a way, she understood their position. She'd basically been their entertainment for years. That had been her designated role in their sibling family. *Cute little Ainsley. Baby.* Always into some silly thing or another. Always messing up. Losing interest in one thing to move on to another.

The way none of them could.

She understood they were only trying to protect her. But sooner or later, they'd have to accept her as an adult. And a capable one at that. "It was an *intro-duction of possibilities,*" she said, trying to convince herself as much as her sister.

"Well, whatever it was, it left Scott worse off than he was before and now something has to be done with him."

Ainsley felt guilty all over again. "I'm not sure something *has* to be done," she began, but the door had closed again and the sound of Miranda's heels quickly faded down the outer hallway.

"Well," Lucinda said. "Aren't we glad she dropped by?"

"She means well," was the only defense Ainsley could offer. She looked again at the message slip and immediately brightened. "Oh, when did Ivan call?"

"Ten, maybe fifteen minutes ago. Right after your sister got here." Lucinda rolled a pencil between her palms. "He wanted to know if you had plans for lunch."

Her spirits rose higher. "I'll have to cancel my dentist appointment."

"I did it already," Lucinda said. "You're free to go…and you don't even have to hurry back. I can hold down the fort while you take an extended lunch break this one time."

"I couldn't ask you to do that, Luce."

"You didn't ask. I volunteered. Now, go. The doctor's waiting for you down on the riverwalk…and you don't want to be late."

Ainsley eyed the receptionist cautiously. "You have something in mind. I can see the wheels turning."

Lucinda's expression turned instantly innocent. "Me? I'm just hoping for a little quiet time alone in the office this afternoon." She began to rearrange items on her desk. "I'm just hoping you'll have a few laughs over lunch, come back relaxed…ready to put together a match."

"A match?"

"Your sister and your friend, the doctor. I mean, if I can't have him and you don't want him, it seems to me you should be shoving your sister right out there as next in line. A little sample of that man's passion could loosen her G-string in a heartbeat."

Chapter Five

"That was fast," Ivan said when Ainsley plopped down beside him on the bench.

"I was motivated," she said. What woman wouldn't be? Lunch on a beautiful day with a good friend who also happened to be a spectacularly fine-looking male?

"You must have been if you managed to wrap up your meeting and get to the riverwalk in less than—" he brought up his wrist in a precise twist and checked his watch "—twelve minutes total."

"Mmm…" She kicked off her shoes and wiggled her toes inside the silky lining of her hosiery, loving the freedom, the cool touch of air on her skin. "It wasn't a meeting. Just Miranda."

"Miranda?"

"She dropped by the office on her way to a lunch date."

"Oh," he said.

But Ainsley was honing her matchmaker instincts

and detected a question in his single-syllable answer. Perhaps a proprietary note, too. "I got your message five seconds after she walked out the door. Otherwise, I'd probably have had to bring her with me."

"You just said she had a date."

Definitely curious, Ainsley decided. "Not a *date*, exactly. More like an appointment over lunch with a hot-shot fund-raiser."

"Oh," he said again. "Guy or gal?"

Definitely interested. Ainsley briefly considered making up a story about the hot-shot fund-raiser being a studly guy instead of a verbose and boring female, just to see if she could detect a hint of jealousy in Ivan's response. But it wasn't worth the chance of getting caught—which she undoubtedly would—so she opted for evasion instead. "What a gorgeous day!" Tipping her head back, she closed her eyes and let the sun warm her face as a soft breeze kicked up off the river to ruffle her hair. "This is soooo much better than the dentist."

He laughed...a wonderfully deep, pleasant sound. "Glad to see I rate right up there at the top of your list."

She kept her eyes closed to better hold on to the sweet warmth in the sunshine, the soothing lap of the river and the lovely relaxation of sitting next to an old friend who loved her just the way she was. "You'll always rate ahead of an appointment to have my teeth cleaned," she said. "No contest."

"That's good to know. I brought lunch, too. Does that bump me up even further in the polls?"

"It gets you an A plus."

"When you find out what I brought for lunch, you'll give me a gold star, too."

"Yum," she said and felt, rather than saw, his immediate smile.

"Aren't you even going to ask what I brought?"

"I don't care—" she said, then clarified "—as long as you haven't developed a taste for rattlesnake steak or cactus soup while you were living out in the great southwest."

"You left out gecko stew."

She wrinkled her nose to that possibility and thought about other lunches she'd shared with Ivan until she hit on one that made her mouth water. "I remember you used to love crabmeat sandwiches, which are also a special favorite of mine."

"Good guess, but that's not what we're having for lunch."

She pushed her lower lip into a pretend pout. "Oh, pooh."

"Nope, today, little lady, we're having—listen for the drum roll here—crabcakes."

That opened her eyes and brought her upright on the bench. "You made crabcakes?" she asked with hopeful enthusiasm. "Really? All by yourself?"

"Just me and the recipe in the tiny kitchen of my temporary digs." He set a brown paper sack on the bench between them. "I've been hungry for some home-cookin' and decided today was as good a day as any to try my hand at it."

Ainsley caught the aroma and her mouth watered with anticipation as she eyed the sack.

He took his time unfolding the top. "You may remember this recipe. I got it a long time ago from—" he paused with one foil-wrapped crabcake halfway out of the bag "—from, um…" he pondered aloud, and it was all Ainsley could do not to reach over and grab her lunch out of his hand.

"Shoot," he said. "I can't remember her name. You know, the chef you had at Danfair when I first came down with Matt for the weekend?" He frowned with the effort of trying to recall the chef's name. "She made these and it was the first time I'd ever even tasted crab, much less crabcakes. They were about the best thing I'd ever tasted and I ate three of them plus half of yours."

"And I didn't stab your hand?"

"No, you handed over your leftovers because I enjoyed them so much. That's what you told me, anyway. You were probably just afraid I was going to eat the plate if I didn't get some more. What the heck was her name?"

"I'm not sure I remember either." Ainsley got another whiff of the spicy aroma and kept her eye on the crabcake, still wrapped, still partially inside the paper sack. "Chefs, like all the rest of the household help, come and go pretty quickly at Danfair, you know. Our house has always been just a stopover on their way to a better life.''

''I know you'd remember this one. She was amazing. Picked up English a lot faster than I could figure out what she was calling the spices she used.'' He snapped his fingers. ''The tiny little Korean woman. Lisa? Lily?''

''Leilana.'' Ainsley snatched her crabcake out of his grasp and was peeling back the foil before he quite realized she had it. ''Her name is Leilana and she stayed with us almost a year. I remember that now. I think she had a bigger crush on you than I did.''

She pinched off a bite of the crabcake and popped it into her mouth, too hungry to wait another second. Her eyes widened, then narrowed with bliss. ''Jeez, this is good. So good, in fact, I could almost believe you had our little Leilana tucked in your pocket.''

He considered her pleasure with a smile. ''When did you ever have a crush on me?'' he asked.

She hesitated, but went on eating—she wasn't about to stop now—and offered only a slight shake of her head in response.

''Come on, Ainsley,'' he prodded as he pulled out another crabcake and began to unwrap it. ''Inquiring minds want to know. You can't say something like that and then drop it.''

''Sure I can.'' She looked around for something to drink. ''These are certainly spicy,'' she hinted.

"That's what makes them so good." He broke off a piece of crabcake and chewed it slowly, before he teased, "Come on now...when, exactly, was this big crush?"

"Obviously, it was while Leilana was learning English at Danfair," she said in a diffident and indifferent tone of voice, as if she wasn't mentally kicking herself for having mentioned her sophomoric crush in the first place. "So it must have been that first year you and Matt were at college together."

"Hmm. And how long did this crush last?" he asked.

She broke off another bite of crabcake. "I imagine only until you tried to weasel all her recipes out of her."

"I was talking about you, not Leilana."

"Mmm-hmm. Did you bring anything to drink?" she asked. "This is making me really thirsty."

"I should have thought of that." He glanced around as if a water fountain might magically appear in front of where they sat. "Wait here. I'll be back." And he left her alone with the crabcakes and the paper sack as he jogged up to street level and out of sight.

Ainsley finished the crabcake in two more bites and, while rubbing her stockinged feet back and forth on the patch of green grass beneath the sun-warmed bench, she pondered why she'd blurted out that she'd once had a crush on him. It had been such a long time ago. She hadn't even thought about it in years, had kept it a secret all this time, only to bring it up now and remind him of what a silly child she'd been when they'd first met. Her thirteen-year-old self had been certain he was a combination of Prince Charming and one—or all—of the Backstreet Boys, the rock star idols of her youth. She'd giggled, blushed and gushed her approval every time Ivan was within fifteen feet of her. Sometimes, even—a lot of times, actually—when he was only there in her imagination.

Surely, he'd known. Miranda had nearly guessed right away, although Matt and Andrew had remained oblivious. Which was a good thing since they'd have teased her unmercifully. She'd decided, early on, that dubbing Ivan her *extra* brother would provide a good cover for her infatuation and keep her family from discovering her true feelings. And over time, she'd come to consider Ivan as more brother than friend.

But not in the beginning. Oh, no. She blushed now, just remembering some of the entries she'd written in her diary back then, extolling Ivan's virtues, his flawless perfection, her plans for their fantasy wedding, the names they'd give to their numerous children. No wonder she'd offered him half of her crabcake. *Smitten* couldn't even begin to describe her state of mind during that phase of her adolescence. She'd been seriously, creatively, in love.

And now he knew.

Even if it shouldn't, *didn't* matter anymore, even

if it ought to be—no, *was*—funny to her now, she didn't much want to be laughing about it with Ivan.

Which was odd, since she loved nothing more than to laugh with him over just about anything.

Already, in the nearly two weeks he'd been back in town, she'd almost told him half a dozen times of her plans to match him with Miranda. She hadn't, of course, proving that she'd learned her lesson about being discreet. But still, the thought was there from time to time…like a delicious conundrum…that if only she could tell him, they'd have a great time planning just how to put the match together.

She pursed her lips and let her gaze travel from her own empty tinfoil to his partially eaten crabcake. He probably wouldn't think it very funny to return from getting her something to drink and find his lunch had disappeared.

On the other hand, smitten or not, she *had* given him half of her crabcake all those years ago.

"FOR YOU," Ivan said, handing her the bottle of water. "I had to talk really mean to the vending machine, but I got it."

She took the bottle eagerly and, twisting off the cap, suckled down a long drink before she gave him a dazzling smile…which more than made up for his frustration with the stubborn vending machine. "Whatever you had to say, Ivan, it was worth it."

"I figured that was how you'd feel about it." He

settled onto the bench beside her again and reached for the rest of his crabcake. The tinfoil crumpled in his hand...empty. Not even a crumb left. His gaze slid to her, tracking his suspicion along with it. "Ainsley? What happened to my crabcake?"

"I think a duck ate it."

He looked up and down the riverwalk, which was—as far as he could see—devoid of ducks. "Must have been a fast one."

She took another swig of the water. "They can fly, you know."

"Right. I should have thought of that."

"Do you want some of my water?" she asked. "I don't mind sharing."

Which was big of her. Considering. "Thank you, yes, I would."

She generously handed him the bottle. "Drink all you want," she offered. "Really. I don't mind."

He was tempted to empty the bottle in one long pull as retribution, but as he raised it to his lips, he tasted a hint of her lipstick—or did the plastic simply retain the scent of her perfume?—and the moment became somehow intimate in a way that startled him. She was smiling at him, her gaze teasing with his, and in self-defense he closed his eyes and tipped the bottle to allow the cool water to trickle down his throat. He felt overly warm all of a sudden, sweaty almost, and there was a suspicious tingling running beneath his skin. There was also an unexpected clutch in his stomach…and, unbidden, he recognized it for what it was.

Awareness.

Which was just plain crazy. This was Ainsley, for Pete's sake. *Ainsley.* He was her *extra* brother. She was like his little sister. He wasn't *aware* of her. It must be her mentioning that she'd once had a crush on him that had him acting like such a…*guy.* Either that or his stomach was just now dealing with the Asian spices he'd put into the crabcakes. Which was the most likely explanation.

Not that he wasn't aware of how—well, *womanly*—she'd become. And it certainly didn't mean he hadn't noticed, couldn't help but notice, the very womanly way she dressed and acted…and yes, looked. But he saw her in the same way he would have looked at Emma had she lived long enough to sit beside him on a bench along the riverwalk…with approval. Pride. He would have been proud of the woman his sister had become. He was proud of Ainsley. That's all this was. A brotherly sort of pride.

"Thanks," he said, handing the bottle back. "I needed that."

"Oh, you're welcome." She squeegeed off the top of the bottle with the palm of her hand and raised it to her lips.

His throat went tight all over again and a renewed sense of awareness knotted inside him as he watched her lower the bottle and lick the moisture from her lips. "Thanks for lunch, Ivan," she said, unaware her extra brother was struggling with a totally inappropriate impulse to kiss her and save her tongue the trouble of getting that last, lingering drop. "Anytime you feel like cooking for me…or the duck…just let me know."

Crossing his arms at his chest in denial, he stared out at the river and took a moment to discipline his wayward thoughts. "You remind me of my little sister," he said, but his voice sounded almost defiant, so he lowered its intensity a notch. "Did you know that?"

"No," she said. "What was she like? Your Emma?"

"Seriously sweet," he said instantly. "Happy. Never a complainer, even though she had plenty of reason."

"Did she look like you?"

The question should have brought Emma's face immediately to mind. But he couldn't seem to bring her into focus. She'd been gone a long time, and it struck him suddenly that he'd known Ainsley longer than he'd known his own sister. "Not really," he answered. "She looked more like my mother." But he didn't know that for certain, and not knowing made him feel anxious, edgy, oddly abandoned.

Turning, he gathered up the aluminum foil and tossed it into the sack. He needed to move around, dispense with this restlessness by walking. Or a long, hard run. "Don't you need to get back to your office?"

"No." She leaned back, as if she had all afternoon, and stretched her willowy legs toward the water. "Lucinda's covering for me, although honestly, since Ilsa's been away, clients aren't exactly beating down the door."

Clients. Men and women looking for love. Marriage. Happily ever after. For no good reason, that thought brought him to his feet. "I feel like walking," he said, springing off the bench. "Let's go."

She squinted up at him. "I know what you're doing, Ivan, and it won't work."

"What am I doing?" he asked, half-afraid she could read his thoughts. His completely insane thoughts. "Trying to help you walk off your lunch? Crabcakes are fattening, you know."

Her blue eyes very nearly snapped at him. "Are you suggesting I *need* to exercise? Because if you are, I only have two words for you."

"And those would be?"

"Dead duck. Now sit back down and let me digest my lunch in peace."

She sounded like a sister scolding a brother. And curiously enough, that unsettled him even more. "I'm a doctor and I think a walk would be a good idea."

Her opinion appeared in the frown lines bunched across her brow. "I'm sitting," she said, closing her eyes in relaxation. "And I really wish you would do the same."

He sat, careful to keep the distance between them neutral—not too close, but not too far, either—and for long moments the silence stretched between them. Gradually, though, by degrees, the nonthreatening lack of conversation and the easy quiet of the interlude tranquilized his lapse into lunacy. What had he been thinking, imagining something that wasn't even there? Getting worked up over thoughts not even fully formed? He'd experienced a simple stomach cramp and reacted as if it were a major shift in his perspective. Next time he'd be a bit less generous with those Asian spices.

"You really shouldn't have eaten my crabcake," he said, the tension slipping away like a shadow on a suddenly cloudy day. "It wasn't a very nice thing to do."

"I know," she said. "I'm sorry." Two planes, traveling in different directions, scored the sky overhead with a wispy vapor trail. "It really wasn't fair, though, to leave me alone with it. You know how susceptible I am to temptation."

"I do," he agreed. "Which is why I ate two before you got here."

"Ivan!"

He laughed, quickly and completely comfortable with her again. The way they always had been. The way he hoped they always would be. "It's Leilana's fault for being such a good cook and for giving me the recipe. I wonder whatever happened to her.''

"She went to culinary school," Ainsley said, a fount of information now that she'd placed the woman. "And recently opened her own restaurant in…Florida, I think. We get letters through the Foundation from practically all of the refugees who've worked at Danfair over the years. Even the ones who only stayed a week or two.''

"I'm certain they're very appreciative of what you all did for them," he said.

"Letting them work for us, you mean?''

"Giving them opportunities they would never have had otherwise," he clarified. "Your folks have always managed to offer a helping hand in the guise of a bargain. A 'we help you…you help someone else,' kind of deal. A 'we'll teach you…you teach another' approach. I don't understand quite how they do it, but they're able to empower one person to help one more and the chain of helping hands keeps fanning out through the world.''

He loved that. It was probably his favorite thing about Charlie and Linney Danville's mission. They believed their responsibility was to help one person at a time and, over the course of their lives, that had translated into helping thousands more that they themselves would never meet. It was the philosophy of the Foundation, their personal creed, and Ivan admired its simplicity and endless, ongoing effect. "I guess I should share the recipe for the crabcakes,'' he said. ''To keep my end of the chain going.''

She slanted a glance at him. ''Yes, you're such a sluggard in that area. Never sharing a bit of yourself with those in need.''

He knew she was teasing, but there was an edge to her voice, an underlying thread of…resentment? But that couldn't be right. Ainsley was one of the most unselfish people he knew. ''I have a long way to go to reach the level your family has cultivated so well.''

''My family has a long history of self-sacrifice,'' she said, and this time it was too definite to be his imagination. Something was bothering her.

''Anything on your mind, Ainsley?''

''No, why?''

But he knew her well and recognized the innocent smile that always appeared to chase the flashes of guilt from her expressive face. ''You just sounded a little edgy, and that isn't like you.''

''It is when I've been with my sister. She's getting really bossy, Ivan. I'm worried about her.''

''Miranda?'' he asked, because the shift of topic had been swift and somehow, pointed. ''What's wrong with Miranda?''

Ainsley sighed dramatically. ''I think she's… lonely.''

''Lonely? Miranda?''

''She hides it well.''

Extremely well, but then Miranda was her sister

and Ainsley probably knew what she was talking about. "I suppose you could be right," he said noncommittally.

She turned toward him on the bench, blue eyes probing. "You think so, too? Has she said anything to you about it?"

The questioning felt just a tad intense. "No, but then I can't imagine Miranda confiding that sort of thing to me."

"But she really likes you, Ivan. I know she does."

This was curious, he thought. "That's good, because I really like her, too."

Ainsley nodded, encouragingly. "Maybe you should talk to her…about being lonely."

"I don't think I'd be comfortable doing that and I'm almost positive she wouldn't be responsive. Not to me."

"Oh, I think you're wrong. I think she'd be more inclined to share her feelings with you than with anyone else."

Now where had Ainsley picked up *that* idea. "I'm not sure that's true, Baby."

She stiffened up like a newly starched shirt. "*Don't* call me that! It's bad enough I can't break the rest of them from thinking I'm still a child, but I thought you, at least, knew better."

"I'm sorry," he said, startled by her vehemence. This wasn't like the Ainsley he remembered, either. "It just slipped out. You know I almost never call you that. However, I do know better and I promise it won't happen again.''

Her head bobbed. ''Thank you. Now, what were we talking about? Oh, yes. Miranda.''

''Miranda,'' he repeated and turned, draping his arm along the top of the seat back, pulling one knee toward the back of the bench so he could face her and gauge her expressions. ''You were talking about Miranda being lonely.''

''Yes. Uh-huh.'' Ainsley's curls caught the sunshine. ''I was saying I think you're the perfect person to talk to her about it.''

This felt a little like one of those conversations in which a patient describes a condition as if another person had it, but in reality it was the someone who was describing the symptoms who actually suffered from the ailment. He considered that possibility, but couldn't see Ainsley as lonely. Or rather, he couldn't believe she would ever see herself as lonely. ''And why do you think I'd be perfect for that?'' he asked, genuinely curious.

''Well, you are a doctor, Ivan, and I'm sure you have a lovely bedside manner.''

''I do,'' he agreed. ''With six-year-olds. But my manner doesn't necessarily translate that well with anyone over twenty.''

''Oh, pooh.'' She smiled widely at him. ''You're just being coy.''

Coy? She thought he was being coy? He was definitely missing something here. "What is this really about, Ainsley?"

She tried hard to look startled, as if she couldn't imagine what he meant. "Miranda," she said as if it ought to be obvious. "Haven't you been paying attention?"

"Yes, as a matter of fact, I have." He held her gaze, hoping she would stop beating around the bush and simply tell him what was on her mind.

But she looked away, instead, and gave a long sigh. "I probably shouldn't have said anything about it, anyway. Just forget I mentioned Miranda at all. Okay?"

"Okay," he agreed, not convinced he should let her off so easily.

"Matt said he gave you the grand tour the other day," she said, nimbly switching the subject. "Did you like the center?"

"I was overwhelmed, to say the least," he admitted readily. "It's a great facility. I can't think of a single thing I'd have done differently with the building."

"There was a lot of discussion about whether or not to include you in the planning stages, but Matt wanted it to be a surprise. He thought if you knew it'd be too much of a distraction."

"He's right. I'd have had trouble keeping my focus on my residency if I'd known what was happening here."

"You've never had trouble keeping your focus,

Ivan.'' She shuffled one stockinged foot against the other, making a soft *shush-shush* sound. ''That's why I sort of hoped you'd say no when Matt called.''

He couldn't believe he'd heard her correctly. ''You don't want me to work for the Foundation?''

''Well, I didn't. Not right away.'' Her feet shuffled some more. ''I wanted you to have some time to enjoy your accomplishment. You know, rest on your laurels for a little while.''

''I don't know how to do that, Ainsley, and I don't believe I want to learn. Not as long as there's hope of helping even one child, of easing the burden for even one family. That's the opportunity your family has offered me and this just isn't the time to rest on my laurels, as you put it.''

''No,'' she said. ''Of course not. I sometimes get these silly ideas. It's probably just as well no one pays much attention to them.'' She didn't allow him a chance to question or contradict her, but instead brightened the afternoon with a sudden flashing smile. ''What did you think of the murals?'' she asked, her voice as enthusiastic as her expression. ''I hoped you'd like them, even if nobody else does.''

''I adore your murals,'' he said. ''Every last funny little creature. I didn't know you were such a gifted artist.''

She laughed. ''There are those who think my artwork is more scribbles than substance. But as long as you like them, I'm happy.''

"They're wonderful, Ainsley. The kids will love them, I guarantee. I expect that second-floor waiting room will become a very popular spot for the patients and a cheerful oasis for their families."

"Miranda said the creatures are weird and will only frighten the children, but Matt wouldn't let her redo them."

"Miranda's wrong," Ivan said. "These kids are fighting demons most adults can't even imagine. They're not going to be scared of your very imaginative drawings."

"I never thought of it like that." Ainsley began wadding up the bag that had held their lunch, crunching it into a brown paper clump. "Did you like the puppet theater? That was my idea, too."

"I know. Matt told me. Another great idea."

"You really think so?"

He smiled at her eagerness for his approval. "Absolutely," he said. "I wish I'd thought of something like it during my residency. The kids in Phoenix would have loved puppet shows."

"I thought it might be a good way for some of your patients to act out their emotions, too."

"Great idea," he said. "Maybe we can find someone—a seamstress, maybe—who can refurbish a regular puppet to look like one of your mural creatures. That could create an interesting puppet show, don't you think?"

She leaned forward to slip on her shoes, smiling at

him over her shoulder. "Let's go for that walk, Ivan."

"Now? Just when I'm getting creative?"

She got up as if she had springs on her feet, then reached back to grab his hand and try to pull him up with her.

A sudden tingling sensation travelled through his fingers and up his arm, unexpectedly reintroducing that odd sense of awareness. But he decided in a heartbeat that this time he wasn't going to overthink the feeling. Whatever its source, he'd never allow it to interfere with his friendship with Ainsley. They had a special relationship and he intended to keep it that way. "What's the hurry?" He allowed her to give his hand a couple of purposeful tugs before he leisurely got to his feet. "A minute ago you thought a walk was a bad idea."

"That was then. Now, it's not." She tossed the crumpled sack into a trash container. "Besides, there's someone I think you should meet."

"I hope it's the duck that ate my lunch."

Her only answer was a sunny giggle.

Chapter Six

Elton wasn't a duck.

Ivan wasn't quite sure what the puppet resembled, but it definitely was not a duck. Jett, on the other hand, was easier to classify. She—Ivan was guessing female because of the huge eyelashes and mop of corded yellow curls—was tiger-striped in varying shades of purple, puce and a rather disconcerting chartreuse. She had a big, bright orange beak—something like a pelican—webbed fingers at the end of each of her four spidery arms, and lips like Madonna. Big, silver hoop earrings and a flower behind her ear—or was that antennae?—defined Jett as the puppet most likely to succeed as a fashion plate. If, of course, puppets wore clothes, which these apparently had no need to do.

Ainsley had brought him to this downtown studio, housed in an old public park building and operated by local artists as a cooperative workshop and gallery, to introduce him to the puppets. All six of them. All destined for the puppet theater at the pediatric center. None of the puppets were the snuggly, big-eyed creatures portrayed in her imaginative murals. No, these characters were more like alien life forms who had chosen body features at random from a variety of earth's species. The puppets—named Elton, Jett, Dodge, Belle, Beau and Hugh—were fascinating works of art and, yes, distinctly charming in their own weird and wacky kind of way.

"Hullo, Dr. Donovan," Elton drawled, coming to lumbering life through Ainsley's low-pitched voice and manipulating hand. "Would ya mind scratchin' my ear?"

Ivan grinned. "Which one?"

Elton, who possessed not one, not two, but three colorful sets of elephantine ears, guffawed. "Any one will do, thanks."

Ainsley patted the puppet's anteater snout and switched characters, picking up the flamboyant Jett. "Well, hello there, Doctor." Jett's purring voice was more giggle than femme fatale, more Gracie Allen than Mae West. "Is that a stethoscope in your pocket or are you just happy to see me?"

Ainsley turned the puppet toward her, frowning down at the blond moppet as if surprised by the character she'd created. "This one is incorrigible," she said, lifting her eyes and her smile to Ivan. "If we ever get her eyelashes batting properly, she's going to cause trouble. I tried to warn Ryan—he's the artist who designed her—but by then it was too late. Jett already had him under her spell.''

As if to confirm this, the puppet's ridiculously long eyelashes blinked down and then up in what could only have been a wink, and Ivan couldn't keep from laughing. ''These are wonderful, Ainsley. How did you manage to do this? I mean, these are really professionally done.'' He paused. ''That didn't come out right. What I was trying to ask is did you do these yourself?'' Frowning, he stopped himself again. ''Okay, that isn't what I meant, either. I know you're amazingly talented, but...'' He pursed his lips. ''Great job, Ainsley,'' he finished.

''I had help,'' she said, coming—belatedly—to his rescue. ''I went to the design school and asked for volunteers, then persuaded the co-op to let us use this space. When all was said and done, there were five students who stuck it out from concept to completion, and a rotating group of local artisans who helped with ideas and materials. They all came through with flying colors, as you can tell. The puppets are a thousand times better than I ever even imagined they could be.''

He was amazed and dazzled by her ingenuity, and her persistence in getting the puppets from idea to two-dimensional life. Although why he should be caught by surprise was a mystery. In the past, Ainsley had often been a source of wonder and pleasant jolts of surprise. From her constantly changing selection of future vocations to the simple wisdom she sometimes voiced with startling insight, she had always managed to fascinate him in one way or another.

But these puppets, along with the mural and the obvious thought she'd put into the projects, touched him in a way nothing else ever had. Maybe it was because the puppets showed, in a special way, her deep understanding of, and compassion for, the children who would soon populate the research center. Young patients who faced life-threatening illness needed fantasy and frivolity more than most. Their lives were overly full of bitter realities and escape wasn't easy to come by...even for half an hour. Ainsley might consider this simply her way of making a contribution, but Ivan believed it was more than that. These well-crafted puppets would form a chain of laughter and cheer that would touch patients and their families, and probably the staff as well. Ainsley had somehow intuited that there was a void, a niche, that her idea could fill.

"Thank you, Ainsley," he said simply. "This is a magnificent gift."

She blushed, understanding all he hadn't said...as she always seemed able to do. "We're working on a wheelchair for Hugh," she said, indicating a puppet whose distinguishing features were a compressed nose like a bulldog's and a head of wavy green grass. "And some type of leg braces that can be put on and taken off easily. The students are fabulous at coming up with new ways to use conduit and plastic tubing, all of which was generously donated through the efforts of the co-op group. You'll be amazed at how little actual money we spent on these guys." Her fingers smoothed Elton's stringy black bangs. "I imagine there are other physical conditions the puppets could exhibit that might help your patients in role-playing, but the wheelchair and leg braces were just the most obvious."

"That's a really good idea," Ivan said. "Would it be okay for me to meet the volunteers sometime and make a few suggestions?"

Her smile signaled her pleasure. "Are you kidding? They'd love to meet you. I've told them what an all-around great brother you are and how you worked so hard to become a pediatric specialist because of your little sister, and how much you were going to appreciate their efforts. When's a good time for you? Evenings or maybe sometime this weekend?"

"Let's do it one evening next week. You choose which one. This weekend, I'm afraid, my dance card is pretty full. Matt's insisting I attend the Denim & Diamonds gala even though he knows socializing isn't my strong suit. I'm going to have to spend all day Saturday practicing my lines."

"Your lines?"

Schooling his expression into a wistful regret, he quoted, "'Would you mind sitting this one out? My tango isn't what it used to be. Old football injury, you know.'" He grinned. "Think that'll work?"

"Old football injury?" she repeated. "You told me you never had time to play sports."

"Well, yeah," he admitted. "But they won't know that."

She conceded the point with a nod. "True, but isn't it going to be a little awkward to ask a woman to dance and *then* tell her about your, uh, injury?"

"Good point. Maybe I'll wait until the women ask me to dance, then give them the line."

"I can think of a couple of women who might take the initiative, but around here the old school of wait-for-the-man-to-ask is still the preferred method of getting a date…or a dance."

"Hmm, I can see I may need to rethink my plan." He ran his hand across his jaw, pretending to contemplate the possibilities. "Any ideas?"

"How about this? You dance a few dances, then sit out a few. That way, you won't get caught fibbing and everyone's happy."

"Except for the women who are unwise enough to take me on as a dance partner."

"Being a great dancer is not necessarily the main requirement in enjoying a dance, Ivan. What woman in her right mind isn't going to be thrilled to be in your arms, not to mention being the focus of your attention for the whole length of a song?"

"The ones with sore feet?"

She dismissed his concerns with a shake of her head. "You're intelligent, handsome and conversant, Ivan. Believe me, I could give you the names of a couple of men I avoid like the plague, even though they're excellent dancers."

"Bucky?" he suggested before he could stop himself.

"I don't avoid Bucky," she said, matter-of-factly. "Although sometimes I'd kind of like to." A frown whisked across her face and vanished into a smile. "Besides, Ivan, I know your secret."

This surprised him. "You do?"

"Uh-huh. I know you *can* dance, but for some reason you don't want to."

"I can Texas two-step," he acknowledged. "And I'm not a complete loss in the country line dances, but put me in a penguin suit in a ballroom and watch out, Mabel…I'm nothing but elbows and left feet."

"Nonsense," she said succinctly. "You've spent too much time studying *Gray's Anatomy* and not enough time studying what's important to the opposite sex. Don't forget who you're talking to here. I remember when you used to dance with me all the time."

"Not all the time. Only occasionally and only when you were a kid and too young to notice that I didn't know what I was doing."

Ainsley cocked her head, mischief lighting her eyes. "You're just being stubborn."

"Realistic," he said.

"Stubborn," she repeated. "And I can prove it. I'll teach you to dance, if you really think you need lessons."

He shook his head. "Not enough time before the gala."

"You see? Stubborn."

If she'd been anyone else, he might have been embarrassed by this discussion, not to mention his lack of grace on the dance floor. But this was Ainsley and her confidence merely made him smile. "Okay, I'll give you a crack at me, but I warn you, your toes will suffer for your persistence."

"I'll take my chances," she said, offering her hand to seal the deal.

He took her hand and gave it a crisp shake and then, suddenly, didn't want to let go. Her hand was small in his and delicate. And he wanted to hold on to it. Maybe forever.

But he didn't.

"So, how soon do we start these tango lessons?" he asked.

"Tango? For someone with a serious lack of confidence in his Fred Astaire persona, you're suddenly pretty ambitious, aren't you?"

"Aha. Now who's trying to waffle out of this deal?" He teased her with a grin, telling himself— again—that he'd only imagined that instant of attraction, that moment when holding her hand had felt just this side of heaven. "But we've agreed, Ms. Danville. You're going to teach me what you know about the art of ballroom dancing, up to and including the dreaded tango. No backing out, now."

Her expressive eyes regarded him thoughtfully as a certain slyness crept into their bluer-than-sapphire sparkle. "You know the person you really need as a partner is Miranda."

"Why? So it can be her feet I step on instead of yours?"

"No, because she's a much better height for you."

"What does height have to do with dancing?"

"Trust me," Ainsley said. "I know what I'm doing."

"Please?" Ainsley leaned in, her hands cupping the front edge of the desk in her sister's office, her expression coaxing, her tone persuasive. "You know you want to."

Miranda never rolled her eyes, but she had a look that managed somehow to convey the same impression. "I've never noticed that Ivan had any particular problem dancing," she said. "He probably doesn't want to attend the event and is using that as an excuse. I can't see how an hour of practicing dance steps with me will do anything to change his mind, and it will certainly put me behind schedule."

Miranda hated getting behind schedule, but Ainsley thought she needed to loosen up a little, throw her day-timer to the wind now and again. Even if she only tossed it a few inches into the air at first. "It's only one evening, Miranda. An hour or so. What if he really is self-conscious about his skills? He says the only dances he remembers how to do are the two-step and some line dances."

"Line dances?"

"Country western. No partners. More wahoo than waltz."

Miranda never sighed, either, but the resigned way she laid her pencil on the landscape drawings in front of her got the idea across. "I have a lot of things to do this evening, Ainsley. Tonight is my last opportunity to go over the final landscape designs for the pediatric center. I want them to be perfect before the crew goes in next week."

"I'm certain those designs—" Ainsley gestured at the sketches "—have been *perfect* for at least a month. You know, Miranda, it is possible to work a project to death. Ivan needs your help. And it's only for a little while."

"Ainsley, I don't see why you need me for this. You can dance with him. You're a much better dancer than I am, anyway."

"This won't work without you."

Miranda's eyes narrowed, suspicion flitted across her expression. "If I were a dance instructor, that might be true. *Might*," she stressed. "But as I'm not,

I believe you can handle the dance lessons all by yourself.''

There were ways to get around Miranda's stubbornness…and Ainsley liked to think she knew them all. ''Come on, Miranda. Just for a little while? I can't dance and give instructions at the same time. I'll have to *stop* the music to explain a step and then *start* the music to show him how to do it. Then I'll have to *stop* the music to explain, and *start* the music to demonstrate. *Stop* the music, *start* the music, *stop* the music, *start* the music, *stop* the music, *start* the music, *stop, start, stop, start*—''

''*Stop!*'' Miranda held up her hand like a traffic cop. ''You're twenty-six years old, Ainsley. When are you going to stop trying to wheedle favors out of me?''

''You're twenty-nine, Miranda. When are you going to stop treating a couple of hours of fun and relaxation as if it's a death sentence?''

Miranda's eyebrows arched in a scold, but her lips were already curving toward a smile. ''One hour,'' she said. ''I'll give you and Ivan one hour after dinner. But that's it, Ainsley. That's time I should be going over these sketches again, so don't pester me for more. Agreed?''

Ainsley nodded and smiled her you're-the-best-sister-in-the-whole-wide-world smile, as she scooted around the desk to administer an affectionate hug. ''Thank you, thank you, thank you. You won't regret this, Miranda, I promise. You may even thank me one day.''

''Don't press your luck, Baby, or I may have you out replanting shrubs to make up for this little favor.'' Miranda's focus turned back to the detailed landscape plans in front of her and Ainsley escaped without having agreed to any time restraints.

She'd replant shrubs with a happy heart if this worked. Not that there was much danger of Miranda having *made* a mistake in her design, and even less that she could have *missed* it all four million times she'd reviewed the layout scheme. The landscape of the new pediatric center would be as well-thought-out as the building itself, a garden of beauty surrounding a hospice of hope.

Despite the sixty minutes of scrutiny Miranda was giving up this evening to dance with Ivan.

Sixty minutes. Ha.

Once she was in Ivan's arms, Miranda would forget she had an agenda. She'd forget the sketches altogether. She'd forget time even existed. Ainsley had danced with Ivan. She knew how it felt.

Miranda wouldn't be able to resist.

MIRANDA DANCED the way she did everything. Precisely. Perfectly. With not a wasted motion or a hair out of place. If that intimidated Ivan, however, he certainly wasn't letting it show. For the past half hour, he and Miranda had danced around the ballroom floor at Danfair with the greatest of ease, proving Ainsley's contention that Ivan could dance when he wanted to and that her sister was the perfect, complementary height for him.

Not that one thing had anything to do with the other. Ivan had a natural grace and, while his steps weren't as polished as say, Matt's, for instance, he had nothing to worry about. As for Miranda's five-foot-eight-inch height...well, Ainsley simply thought she fit well with Ivan's six-foot-three-inch frame.

Not that *that* mattered, since neither one of them seemed even remotely aware of how good they looked together.

From the sidelines over by the open terrace doors, Ainsley observed her sister and her friend with a critical eye as they swirled past on the three-quarter rhythm of a waltz. How could two people who were so dead-on perfect for each other seem so blithely unaware of the romantic potential between them? Just what was it going to take to get these two to notice the possibilities in each other? Where was the spark of attraction and when was it ever going to ignite?

"Keep your arms bent, but relaxed," Ainsley instructed as they circled close to her again.

"He's doing fine," Miranda said in crisp tones that irritated Ainsley more than usual. "Quit fussing at him."

"I was talking to you," Ainsley fired back in sisterly rebuttal. But, of course, Ivan really was the one she'd been trying to coach from the sidelines, for reasons that were foggy even to her. It was clear he didn't need much in the way of guidance. He was doing fine, getting whatever subtle corrections he might require from his dancing partner, the multitalented Miranda. But the longer Ainsley watched them the more she wished she'd never asked her sister to help. The more blended their dance steps became, the more she regretted putting them together like this. Talk about wasted opportunities. This was almost as bad as watching Scott walk right past his perfect match and sit down at the table with Molly.

The more Ainsley thought about it, the more annoyed she became. She was starting to wonder if Ilsa's method of researching a client and then setting up an *introduction of possibilities* wasn't outdated. Maybe there was something to be said for arranged marriages and introducing the two main participants after they'd already exchanged vows. Then a matchmaker would really be in charge and there'd be none of this frustrating waiting around for something— *anything*—to happen.

Why she was so impatient with the pace of this particular romance, Ainsley couldn't quite decide. Maybe she was simply overeager to jump ahead to the conclusion of this drama…or nondrama, as it was turning out to be. Or maybe she was restless and wanted a change, needed something new to think about. Maybe she knew the players too well. But there was no avoiding the knowledge that if Miranda would open her eyes and *look* at Ivan, there'd be no further need for a matchmaker. And if Ivan would pay some serious attention to the woman he currently held in his arms, he could have her heart on a string before the "Blue Danube" came to its final harmonic chord.

Earlier, Ainsley had thought this dance practice was one of her better ideas. The perfect opportunity for one of those oh-my-what-have-I-been-missing? moments, with the added benefit of not being a true *introduction of possibilities.* If there had been even a little bit of cooperation from either one of the primary parties tonight, Ainsley could later truthfully claim to Ilsa—or even Miranda, if the subject ever came up—that she hadn't, technically, done anything to put together the match.

Ivan had needed a refresher course.

Miranda was an excellent dancer.

Voilà, the whole thing had simply happened during the dance lesson, she could say. She'd be off the hook professionally and not accountable for the eventual outcome. She could be pleasantly surprised when the romance developed, and delighted as it progressed.

But that wasn't happening.

Nothing was happening…except that she was feeling more and more like a star player, confined to the bench, while the second-string athletes lost the game.

"There, that was perfect," Miranda said as they glided to a stop on the final note of the waltz. Then, without so much as a blink of reluctance, she stepped back out of his arms.

Ainsley just had time to wonder if her sister was actually conscious, before Ivan turned to her with a question. "What do you think, Ainsley?" he asked. "Am I ready for Broadway?"

Miranda laughed, displaying her rarely exercised sense of humor. "Just like a man. Once around the floor without mishap and he's ready to star in a musical."

Personally, Ainsley thought Ivan would be terrific…it was her sister she worried about.

"Maybe I need a little more practice before the auditions start," he conceded with a grin. "I did warn you, Miranda, I have more enthusiasm than finesse."

"You'll do fine at the gala," Miranda said confidently. "But my advice is to concentrate on the basics and leave the *finesse* for a later occasion."

"You two were mad to dance together," Ainsley said, believing—however futilely—that the evening might still be redeemed. "Why don't you dance one more dance together before we quit."

"Oh, I think being *mad* to dance together is a fitting conclusion to this lesson," Ivan said, picking up on her slip of the tongue and teasing her with a grin. "And I'm sure Miranda's relieved to have it over."

"You weren't that bad," Miranda said.

"Made," Ainsley corrected even though they

weren't listening. "I meant to say you were *made* to dance together."

"Thanks for working with me, Miranda. I do feel a little more confident now, and if all else fails, I have a line ready to go."

"Let me guess—" Miranda said "—old football injury?"

"How did you know?"

"Experience."

"Miranda used to date a football player," Ainsley supplied, although no one had asked her. "Nick Shepard."

"Good old Nicky," Miranda said. "He used that 'old football injury' excuse any time he didn't want to do something. Which happened quite a bit, as I recall."

"He's still a great-looking guy, though. He's on television now. A soap opera star," Ainsley said, which was not only irrelevant but downright dumb.

Miranda seemed a little puzzled by it, too, but whatever she might have said in response was interrupted by Tomas, who stood in the doorway, shifting his weight from foot to foot, unsure if he could speak before being spoken to, no matter how many times he was told otherwise.

"Yes, Tomas?" Miranda asked.

"Telephone," he said, turning it into a foreign word with about six extra syllables, a cross between his native language and the English he was learning with painstaking effort. "For you."

"Me? For Miranda?" Miranda pronounced her name distinctly, as she always liked to be sure before she took a call that it was, actually, for her. No wrong numbers allowed on her time.

Tomas nodded, pleased to have gotten his message across on the first try. "Meez Murr-an-da," he repeated. "Where take?"

"Well done, Tomas, thank you. I'll take the call in the study."

He smiled and nodded some more as he backed from the doorway. Miranda was halfway to the door herself before she seemed to remember her manners. "I enjoyed our dance, Ivan," she said. "I'll see you Saturday night."

"I'll understand if you want to sit out our dance," he called after her.

"Don't be silly," she called back, and was out the door and gone.

Good riddance, thought Ainsley, the forgotten.

"Well, I think that went well," Ivan said.

"Oh, it was just hunky-dory."

"You don't think I'm ready for prime time, huh?"

Chagrined at allowing her pique with Miranda to show, she offered a smile to offset it. "I think you were ready before my sister even walked into the room, but then Miranda's opinion always carries more weight than mine."

Not her best effort at hiding her feelings. Ainsley turned on her heel and walked over to fiddle with the sound system. Her hands shook a little and that agitated her all the more. There was no reason for her to be upset. Just because she had a sister who might as well be in a coma for all the attention she paid to the possibilities right in front of her nose. But why should Ainsley care? It wasn't as if tonight had been some kind of final exam she had to take before becoming a full-fledged matchmaker. There wasn't an exam. Not even a test case. Ilsa would never even know about this. *No one* would ever know about it…because *nothing* had happened.

"Ainsley? Is something bothering you?"

She glanced over her shoulder, schooled her expression into unconcern. "Me?" she asked, feigning innocence. "No. What would be bothering me?"

"I don't know. That's why I asked."

"No," she said brightly. "Nothing."

"So what are you doing?"

"Turning off the music." Except that the music hadn't stopped although she was pressing—and pressing—the off button.

He reached for her hand, pulling it away from the control panel. "You're hitting the dimmer switch," he said.

Only then did she notice the lights were fading around the perimeter of the ballroom. "Oh, well, I was close. The sound system is right…'' She leaned forward to squint at the panel of switches.

''Over there.'' Ivan indicated another panel nearly a foot away from the first.

''I knew that.'' Pretending she wasn't flustered by her mistake, Ainsley reached over and tapped Eject. Like magic, the music stopped, and with a highly calibrated whir the CD tray slid open. She should have just hit Off, she realized. ''Oops, didn't mean to do that.''

Her over-the-shoulder glance caught Ivan's puzzled expression. ''Are you sure you're okay?'' he asked.

''I'm terrific. Are you sure *you're* okay?''

''I'm fine.''

''Great.'' She returned to contemplating the CD tray…and the reason her heart was hammering her rib cage insistently and her palms were beginning to sweat. Being upset with Miranda wasn't exactly something new. They were sisters, after all, and living under the same roof, albeit a very large roof. But their disagreements didn't usually leave Ainsley this agitated, this unfocused. She couldn't figure it out, unless maybe she was coming down with something.

''Can I help?''

She jabbed a few buttons and the rack slid back into place. ''I'm changing the music,'' she said decisively. ''Let's tango.''

Surprise arched his brow as she spun to face him,

extending her arms for the dance. "I thought we just decided I should stick to the basics."

"That was Miranda," she said. "Given a choice, she'll always opt for the basics. I, on the other hand, think people ought to take a risk now and then, if only to speed up their metabolism." Ainsley grabbed his hands and placed them in position, one at her waist, one at her shoulder. "Are you ready?"

"I think that should be my line."

"Dance," she commanded, and on the downbeat of the music she propelled him back and into the steps.

To say he picked up the intricate footwork with little effort would have been a misstatement. But he took his cues from her, and although he did falter occasionally, there was no denying he had an innate sense of timing and anticipated her moves with surprising accuracy. Numerous times in the past, she had coaxed him into twirling her around this very ballroom floor. They'd laughed and teased and paid no attention whatsoever to their feet. Even less to what dance step they were improvising. It had been movement, an expressive joy in the moment, and nothing more. They'd been simply two friends—brother and sister, really—clowning around.

But this wasn't like that.

Something had changed. She didn't know what. Or why. But this wasn't like that, at all.

She was too short for him. He was too tall for her.

But somehow, the longer the dance went on, the more perfectly their moves coalesced and the easier it became to lose herself in the dance, in the warmth of his hands as they pulled her close, then spun her away again. She was conscious, in a way she hadn't been before, that he was not her brother, that he was, in many ways, a stranger. Her heart—kickstarted by her agitation even before the music began—jumped several beats at that realization, and she stumbled.

He caught her easily and swept her back into the dance, a certain rueful determination in the smile he offered, as if the misstep had been his fault. She knew it had been hers, yet she didn't say so. For the first time in memory, she didn't know what to say to Ivan, didn't have the words to explain her odd thoughts and feelings. They pulsed inside her body, as if the music had gotten into her blood and made it pound with a rhythm not her own. Her palms were no longer sweating—they felt dry as a desert now…and hot. Her fingers felt tingly, too, but when she flexed them, it only seemed to increase their sensitivity.

"Okay?" she asked Ivan, forcing the word into a bright inquiry, as if she were simply worried that he might be, somehow, not okay.

"Great," he said, and his voice sounded normal, as if this was no different than all those other times he'd danced with her in this room. "How about you?"

She nodded, unable somehow to meet his eyes, definitely incapable of conversing with him. This was ridiculous. Her imagination must simply be running with all the things she'd hoped would happen with Miranda. She was just playing her sister's role, that was all, allowing this dance to take on an importance it wouldn't otherwise have had. That was the reason everything felt topsy-turvy. That was why dancing with Ivan seemed suddenly so fraught with danger. With *possibilities*.

Ainsley missed another step, but recovered in time to dip backward across his arm. For a split second, she got lost in his gaze, in the enigma of wondering what might have happened had she been Miranda and awake to the possibilities of him. Would he have kissed her in that moment? Would she have kissed him?

The music surged and Ivan pulled her up and back into the dance, unaware—thankfully—of how wild her thoughts had been. This was crazy. She wasn't Miranda, who had probably never done an impulsive thing in her whole life. She was Ainsley, whose imagination had always hovered closer to fancy than fact. Next thing she knew she'd be imagining that he *had* kissed her.

The idea took root, despite her effort to shake it. Fighting it proved futile, considering the unavoidable intimacy of the dance and the impossible explanation it would require to simply stop. So, as a last resort, she let her imagination go, allowed herself to wonder if Miranda would like Ivan's kiss. Which led straight into a question of what, exactly, his kiss would be like.

Closing her eyes, Ainsley imagined she was her sister and only seconds away from experiencing Ivan's kiss. It would be slow in coming—that much she knew. And tender, perhaps even tentative in that first touch of his lips to hers. Miranda wasn't an easy woman to approach on any terms, after all. But that first brush of lips would wipe out her resistance and from there...well, Ainsley imagined that from there the kiss would deepen quickly, thoroughly, banishing inhibitions with ease. In combination, there would be the sensation of strong arms pulling her against a muscular body, the willingness of her own body to melt into his, the heady rush of timelessness. Maybe weightlessness, too. The loop of desire that started low and spiraled up, weaving passion into the embrace, building intensity into the kiss. Ainsley's palms began to sweat again and she caught her tongue darting anxiously, eagerly, feeling the subtle tremor of her own suddenly aching lips.

"Ainsley? Are you sure you feel okay?"

She snapped out of the dreamlike trance with a disconcerting blink and realized they were no longer dancing. "What?" she asked, the word coming out in an embarrassingly throaty purr. "W-what?" she repeated, struggling to recover her equilibrium.

He regarded her intently, obviously concerned.

"Are you sure you're okay? You seem sort of… dazed."

She pushed back out of his arms, had the sudden, silly urge to shake herself from head to toe, like a dog coming inside out of the rain. "See?" she said, although she couldn't get her mind around what she wanted to point out.

"See?" he repeated. "See what?"

She lifted her chin. "See, you *can* dance."

His smile seemed normal, relaxed, as if this dance had been no different than any other. Which it hadn't been, except in her imagination. "Oh, yeah?" he teased, sounding just like one of her brothers. "Says who?"

"Me," she said, offering up a flippant smile, reality returning not a moment too soon. "Your little sister."

And that was exactly the way it was supposed to be.

AINSLEY HEARD a soft footfall and recognized it as Andrew's, a moment before he drew back the curtain and found her in the window seat of the nursery they'd once shared. If he was surprised to see her, it didn't show. But then, the two of them had discovered this hidden alcove as children and, through the years, it had become their thinking place. The window, which they'd figured out how to unlatch when they were eight or nine, opened outward and they'd spent a lot of hours since, both together and separately, watching the sky and contemplating their personal dilemmas.

"Hi," Andrew said, taking his place on the opposite wall. He was almost too big to fit, although the window seat was wide, but he drew his knees up to his chest and clasped his arms loosely around them, his head turned toward the star-studded sky.

Ainsley was in a replica of his pose, knees drawn to her chest, arms clasped around them, her eyes studying galaxies far away. It didn't seem the slightest bit strange that he had found her in their alcove tonight. Nor did it seem odd that he would sit across from her, lost in his own thoughts, but attentive somehow to hers, too. They were brother and sister, no more alike than Matt and Miranda, yet they were closer in ways neither of them could explain. He often sensed that she was troubled before she was quite aware of it herself. She knew at times he was leaving on a trip before he'd even made the decision to go. He knew when she needed someone to listen. She knew when he needed her quiet companionship. The mysterious bond of being twins existed between them as adults as surely as it had when they were still children. And tonight, Ainsley was grateful that he'd found her, whether he'd come to the alcove because he thought she needed him there or to ponder a problem of his own.

He inhaled a slow, deep breath of night and asked, "Got something on your mind?"

"Maybe," she answered. "What about you?"

"Maybe." He was quiet for a while. "I'm leaving for Salt Lake City in the morning," he said. "It's a shoot for *Restaurant Review*. Five featured chefs. Shouldn't take more than three or four days."

"Are you taking Hayley?"

"I asked if she'd like to go, to get some experience in food photography, but she said no. She seemed so relieved I wasn't going to make her go, I think she almost hugged me in gratitude. But she ran into the bathroom instead and stayed in there for half an hour." He paused long enough for his curiosity to grow into a baffled question. "Do you think I intimidate her that much? My former assistants have pestered me to death wanting to go on a magazine shoot. *Any* magazine shoot. If she's that scared of me, why doesn't she quit and work for someone else? With her portfolio, she could easily find another position."

Ainsley laid her head on her knees, stared at a single star until it blurred into another. "Miranda and I gave Ivan a refresher course in ballroom dancing tonight," she said. "He hadn't forgotten as much as he thought he had."

"Hayley says while I'm gone she'll work on printing some black-and-whites for an art class she's taking."

"Ivan and Miranda looked really good dancing together. They're the right height for each other." Ainsley couldn't get the image of them dancing out of her head. Or rather, she kept having to haul it out to replace the memory of her own dance with Ivan.

''Why is she taking an art class? In photography, of all things? Doesn't she think my prints qualify as art?''

''Miranda wasn't very interested.'' Ainsley still couldn't figure it out. She'd been so sure that dancing together would spark an attraction. Why hadn't Miranda fallen into the sensual fantasy Ainsley had found so easy to conjure for her? ''The landscape plans for the new center go to the crew next week and she's afraid there will be a mistake on them somewhere. A mistake. Can you imagine our sister making a mistake?''

''There's a practical side to photography, you know.'' Andrew's voice was picking up an edge of irritation. ''There's artistry involved in every photo, but every photo doesn't necessarily have to qualify as art. I have yet to even see her pick up the digital camera. You'd think she'd want to see what she can do with it. But no. She likes film. She likes to work in the darkroom. Alone.''

''Maybe I don't know what I'm doing,'' Ainsley said. ''Maybe I have no business trying to be a matchmaker.''

''Maybe Miranda and Ivan aren't a match,'' Andrew said, his musings merging into her conversation.

''Maybe Hayley is afraid she's not good enough to

work with you,'' Ainsley said, her thoughts circling back to his problem.

''Maybe you're trying to do something that doesn't need doing.''

''Maybe you should ask Hayley what she hopes to learn from being your assistant.''

A soft breeze blew in from the ocean, ruffled the curtains behind them.

''I'm hungry,'' Andrew said. ''Let's raid the kitchen.''

Ainsley smiled. ''The new chef will complain to Miranda, you know, when he discovers we've been pillaging his supplies. He seems a little on the temperamental side.''

Andrew shrugged. ''Miranda's too busy worrying about her landscape design to think about anything else.''

At that moment, Ainsley loved being a twin, loved having someone who could get her mind off of dancing with Ivan and sharing imaginary kisses with the man who was a perfect match for her sister.

''That's right.'' Ainsley swung her legs down from the window seat. ''And if she does ask about any missing food, I'll tell her you must have taken it with you.''

He grinned. ''Tell her I needed it for a photo shoot.''

''You bet I will.''

They laughed together and headed for the kitchen.

Chapter Seven

Ivan escaped the gaiety of the Denim & Diamonds
gala inside and sought out a moment's privacy on the
beautiful back terrace of Rosecliff Mansion. There
were several other guests with the same idea, but they
seemed no more inclined to disturb his respite than
he was tempted to intrude on theirs. He found a vacant spot along the terrace wall from which to admire
the grandeur of Rosecliff's night-flooded garden. He
soaked in the distant, rhythmic sounds of the ocean
lapping against the cliffs and inhaled the elusive scent
of rain somewhere out at sea.

Who would have thought that a native Texan, born
and raised on the theory that bigger was better, would
find a Texas-size affection for the smallest state in the
USA? But being back in Newport, breathing in the
salty air of the Atlantic, Ivan felt as if he'd come
home after a long journey. He'd been away a full five
years, the entire length of his internship and residency. He'd had neither time, energy nor the extra

money for a visit to the East Coast and he'd told himself it was the memories he missed, believed he was simply nostalgic for the good times he'd spent at Danfair, the relative simplicity of his life before he'd plunged his energies into becoming a specialist in the field of serious pediatric illnesses.

But now that he was here again, he could no longer deny that here was where a part of his heart had stayed all along.

"Great night, isn't it?" Matt joined him on the terrace, handed him a drink, shared the view of the night sky. "Although that bank of clouds looks like rain is headed our way."

"I don't believe a little rain will dampen spirits tonight." Ivan lifted his glass. "By the sound of the crowd inside, I'm guessing this fund-raiser is a success."

Matt shrugged. "The Denim & Diamonds gala is usually one of our better events. A couple of months ago it was the Black and White ball, which is always popular. Two months from now, we'll have the Danville Regatta. Then there's the Laps for the Little Ones run, the Green is Great golf tournament, and the Harvest gala in the fall. And that's not counting the various small receptions and lunches we have in-between. It amazes me sometimes that each of the fund-raisers continue to do so well."

"The Danville Foundation supports one of the best causes in the world," Ivan said. "Children. The money goes to feed them, provide medical care for them, build houses for them to sleep in and helps their family. It gives hope for the future. That's a great exchange for the cost of a few hours of entertainment.''

"One night in a tuxedo, surrounded by women who are panting for your attention, and you've changed your mind about socializing for the greater good?''

"Not a chance. You know I'd rather be working.''

"You are working, Ivan. You're making a good impression and that's an invaluable asset for the pediatric center and the Foundation. I predict we'll receive a contribution or two from the parents of at least one eligible debutante who sees you as the answer to her prayers.''

Ivan laughed. "I doubt that. I may be a bachelor, but I doubt many of the parents in there would think my west Texas credentials are a good match for their daughter's.''

"You've always been overly conscious of your middle-class background, Ivan. Any family represented here tonight would be crazy not to want you for an in-law.''

He wasn't even conscious of having the thought before he heard himself asking, "Even the Danvilles?''

"*Especially* the Danvilles.'' Matt turned to look at him. "Are you saying you're interested in a long-term relationship with my sister?''

Ivan shook his head. "I don't know where that came from, Matt. I'll admit that there was a time when I had a serious case of infatuation with Miranda. I mean what red-blooded male wouldn't? She's beautiful, smart, and what my high school buddies would have referred to as a filly with a stripe, a strip and four white stockings. For you Yankee folks, that's Texan for a prime filly."

Matt grinned. "I can't imagine anyone who knows Miranda using that particular phrase to describe her. I'm almost positive she wouldn't find it flattering." He sipped his drink. "So what stopped you from dating her back when you had this serious case of infatuation?"

"I didn't want to risk your friendship," he said simply. "Plus I could tell she wasn't interested."

"I don't know. It's always hard to tell with Miranda." Matt rattled the ice in his highball glass. "I can't believe you ever thought for a second I'd mind if you dated my sister. Maybe you should ask her out now."

The idea had absolutely no appeal. None. Ivan rejected the fleeting thought that dating Ainsley did. "What are you?" he asked Matt with a teasing grin. "The apprentice matchmaker's assistant? Isn't putting two and two together Ainsley's job?"

"I was only thinking that if you were my brother-in-law, I wouldn't have to worry about losing you to one of those headhunters who keep calling you with other job offers.''

''How do you know about that?''

''Connections. One of the perks of being a Danville.''

''One of the perks of being my best friend is that I'll tell you honestly that there isn't an enticement great enough to lure me away from here. You've offered me the opportunity to do what I've always wanted to do—research and treatment for kids like my sister, who need a cure yesterday, not tomorrow. Believe me, Matt, I'm not going anywhere.''

''Someday this might not be all you want, Ivan.''

''I can't imagine that, but if it happens, we'll talk about it then.''

A couple came out onto the terrace and moved past Matt and Ivan into the shadows of the garden, seeking seclusion. They were so lost in their private conversation, so wrapped up in each other, they didn't even notice the people they passed. Ivan watched them go, feeling a breath of loneliness brush across the back of his neck and spin away. ''We should go back inside,'' he said. ''It sounds like they're about to start the after-dinner acknowledgments and your absence, if not mine, would undoubtedly be noted.''

Matt finished his drink. ''So speaks my newest recruit to the cause of politically correct fund-raising.'' He clapped Ivan on the back. ''Let's go, Doctor. If you're sure I can't persuade you to try your hand with

Miranda, there are a couple of other women you might like to meet.''

''I never needed your help to meet women before,'' Ivan commented. ''What makes you so anxious to offer your assistance now?''

''Just think of it as me steering you toward the prime fillies, Tex. Call it a perk of being my best friend.''

Ivan grinned and the two men left the terrace for the bright lights inside.

''I'M DOING OKAY,'' Scott said, although he clearly wasn't.

Ainsley tipped back her glass of water, taking as big a swallow as was ladylike under the circumstances. The circumstances being that she was wearing a spectacularly form-fitting evening gown of shiny, denim-blue with more silvery beads than stretch, while standing next to the bar at the Denim & Diamond gala, listening to her cousin tell her in a soft, miserable voice for the fourth time that he was fine. Just fine.

''It's not been even a month, Scott,'' she said. ''No one expects you to be feeling on top of the world.''

''Easy for you to say. You don't have to listen to my father telling me what a lucky escape I had, how I ought to thank my lucky stars that girl—he always calls her *that girl* like she was just anybody—hightailed it before she said, 'I do,' and put me to the trouble of getting an annulment.''

Ainsley sighed, wondering if she was ever going to stop feeling guilty about this. "I'm sure Uncle Edward means well."

Scott sniffed, picked up a glass of wine for the third time, then set it back down—for the *third* time—without taking a drink. "Probably."

"Maybe she'll get in touch with you," Ainsley suggested, wanting to offer words that might cheer him up. "At least offer you some explanation for what happened."

He hung his curly red head, his chin dipping toward his chest. "I know where she is," he all but whispered.

This was news. Ainsley set her glass on the bar and nodded to the waiter for a refill. Across the length of the ballroom, the evening's MC—Jeb Strider, co-chair of the gala with his wife, Patti—was winding up the formal program by thanking everyone for their support and preparing to hand out the final award of appreciation. Many of the guests were still seated at the tables where they'd been served dinner, but several were up milling around, restless from sitting, chatting quietly with friends, waiting for the dance to begin. "Where is she?" Ainsley asked. "How did you find her? Have you talked to her?"

Scott merely shrugged, as if none of that mattered. "She's in Florida, or at least she was. I kept phoning her aunt, hoping to get a clue as to somewhere, any-where, she might have gone. And the last time I called—last Thursday—Molly answered the phone.''

''What did she say?''

''Nothing. When she realized it was me, she hung up...and since then, I get nothing but a busy signal.''

''But if she's there, that means she didn't elope with the bartender, like you thought.'' Ainsley had never actually believed Molly had done any such thing, but she seriously wanted to help her cousin feel better. ''That's good, right?''

''He could be there with her, for all I know.''

''Have you checked to see if he's still working at the restaurant? Have you thought about going to Flor-ida to see her?''

''What's the point? I need to face reality, like Dad says. Molly didn't want to marry me.''

''Maybe she was scared.'' Ainsley patted his arm, feeling guilty all over again for her part in his misery, wanting to fix it somehow, reminding herself of Ilsa's advice to let Scott work out his own solution. ''Maybe it all happened too fast and she got scared.''

Scott shrugged. ''It doesn't matter.'' Although it was clear that it did.

The audience applauded with a collective vigor that signaled the end of the presentations, and Ainsley clapped, too, before accepting her newly refilled glass. She took a slow sip of the water and pondered what she could say to make her cousin feel a little less miserable. "Maybe this will work out for the best," she offered lamely.

"Yes," he agreed without enthusiasm. "That's what my father keeps saying, too…except he doesn't add the 'maybe.'"

It was true, Ainsley knew. The family had switched sides after Molly's desertion. Where she'd been deemed entirely suitable for Scott before she'd left him at the altar, everybody now claimed the match had never been a good idea. "Give it time, Scott," she advised. "Things have a way of working out."

"Sure they do," he tried to sound brighter, hopeful. Unsuccessfully, but at least it was the most effort he'd displayed since their conversation had begun. "You're a matchmaker, Ainsley," he said, suddenly, desperately clutching her arm. "Do you think there's any hope Molly will ever speak to me again?"

She didn't know. She really didn't. But that was not what he wanted, needed, to hear. "If that's what you want, Scott, I'm sure she will. Eventually. If you give her some time to think things through."

"I just need to know she's happy," he said. "Even if it's not with me."

The hangdog look had returned, worse than before, and Ainsley had to do something. "You know, maybe you'd feel better if you asked someone to dance. Got your mind off of Molly for a little while. What about that nice Shelby Stewart?"

"Who?" he asked, although Ainsley knew he had met Shelby on at least one other occasion.

"Shelby Stewart," she repeated. "I think she's always had something of a crush on you."

That was a little desperate sounding, Ainsley thought, but she smiled as if she believed what she'd just said. "Why don't you go over and ask her to dance?"

He frowned. "I'd look really stupid asking a girl to dance before the band gets started. Besides, you know I'm not very comfortable on the dance floor."

"Ask her to sit one out with you, then."

"Oh, right, like she's going to want to do that."

Ainsley was growing a trifle impatient with feeling guilty. Maybe Scott didn't *want* to feel better. "Tell her you have an old football injury."

He looked at her as if she'd lost her mind. "She'd never believe I got injured playing football."

Which was probably true. "Shelby's very nice," she said in a last-ditch effort to coax him into stepping outside the box. "She's pretty. She's smart. I think you'd like her. She might be just what you need to forget your troubles."

He looked across the room where smart, pretty, likable Shelby was sharing a laugh with her father. "She's not Molly," he said.

And that, apparently, was that. Ainsley gulped the rest of her water and decided she'd go to the ladies' room and powder her nose. Or fix her lipstick. Or just hide out until Scott had taken his sad, defeated attitude and looked for comfort somewhere else. She felt badly about deserting him. She felt badly about having botched up his romance in the first place. She even felt badly about trying to fix him up with Shelby again. But her feeling badly obviously wasn't doing one darn thing to help Scott feel any better. "Things will work out, Scott," she said. "I believe that. I hope you can, too."

"Thanks," he said in a half-hearted way, and picked up his neglected wineglass again.

Leaving him at the bar, Ainsley began to make her way toward the ladies' room, half wishing she'd had wine instead of water. Not that alcohol and misery were ever good companions. She did wish Ilsa were back from her trip and here to advise her on how she might have helped her cousin. At the moment, she was sorely tempted to catch a midnight flight to Florida and drag Molly back here to face the heartache she'd left behind.

Of course, taking that kind of action would be matchmaker interference of the highest order...and therefore, against the rules. Not to mention an all-around bad idea.

"Excuse me," Ainsley said, as she skirted past a tight cluster of people in the midst of the crowd. Now that the program was over, everyone was up and moving around, which necessitated some maneuvering. The ballroom at Rosecliff, another Newport mansion, was long and narrow, large enough to handle tonight's crowd, but not without something of a walk to reach one of the powder rooms.

Ainsley loved all of the Newport mansions, although Danfair, of course, was her favorite. Danfair was still a private home, as opposed to a public treasure, and wasn't open for tours and events. Her parents had been surprisingly adamant that Danfair should be their children's haven, where they were free to be whomever they chose. Over the years, Ainsley had come to understand that Danfair was the reason Charles and Linney could leave their children behind with such equanimity. Her parents loved the house and its gardens, defined the view as the most beautiful they'd ever seen, and the landscape as peaceful as Heaven surely must be. They trusted the house in a way that was both puzzling and purposeful, and they had a serene faith their children were safe there.

And so it had turned out to be.

Ainsley wondered if her parents would retire from their mission trips and live again at Danfair, but somehow she couldn't picture them settled, content to spend the last years of their lives simply looking at the view. They'd work until they dropped… wherever that happened to be. The house would be donated to the Preservation Society and, sometime in the future, perhaps, tourists would wander through the rooms at Danfair, imagining the family that once had lived there.

Or more likely, her parents would eventually want Danfair to become an extension of the Foundation. A halfway house for refugees or a place of shelter for those seeking asylum. Even a school, perhaps. Ainsley couldn't even imagine all the opportunities her home might someday provide.

It was sort of odd to think about not living there with her brothers and sister. On the other hand, they'd all have families of their own at some point. They wouldn't live at Danfair forever. Well, Matt might, she supposed. For her part, Ainsley wouldn't mind moving away from Newport entirely. Perhaps to another part of the country. Somewhere The Danville Foundation wouldn't be so endlessly present in her life.

Reaching the smaller of the ladies' rooms, Ainsley was surprised and relieved to find it deserted. As the outer door swung shut behind her, she stepped in front of the double mirror and eyed her reflection critically. Was she really that selfish? she wondered. The Foundation did great things. Her parents accomplished more good in the world than they ever acknowledged. Giving was in her blood. It was her heritage. But more and more, Ainsley struggled with the compromise her parents had made, continued to make. She'd had a charmed life, she knew, but that didn't erase the fact that she'd grown up virtually an orphan, with her parents more often a voice on the other end of the phone than a genuine presence in her life. She didn't want her children to grow up that way. She didn't want them ever to feel they were unimportant to her or to wish they had known her better. She didn't want them to have to wonder where they fit in. She wanted a husband and children and a life that belonged only to her.

Was she the only Danville to ever feel that way? Uncle Edward hardly ever left New England. He managed the family's personal investments, spearheaded new financial and commercial ventures, which increased the Danville fortune, which in turn brought more money into the Foundation's coffers, which in turn financed the good works her parents were able to do.

If she had a head for business, she could follow in her uncle's footsteps…none of his children seemed to have the slightest inclination to do so. Or if she'd been a take-charge organizer like Miranda, she could play a role in planning the Foundation's future. As smart as Matt, and she could oversee projects and investments, evaluate requests, suggest new areas of aid and help ensure the Foundation functioned successfully in an ever more complex world. As brave as Andrew, or as talented, maybe she would have wanted to travel and help document the Foundation's good works.

But she was just Ainsley. The baby of the family, who felt selfish because she didn't want the Foundation to be her whole life. The Danville who wanted to be a matchmaker and change the world of one man and one woman, one love story at a time.

Unfortunately, she couldn't even claim she had much talent for that. Otherwise, her cousin wouldn't be out there, now, telling some other sympathetic ear that he was okay. Fine, just fine.

Studying her reflection, she could see her nose did need powder and her lips could stand some color. But she had nothing with her to do a repair job. She had trouble keeping up with a purse at these functions, so she never brought one. Forethought...also not her strong suit.

Miranda came through the door. "I thought I saw you dart in here," she said, moving to stand beside Ainsley in front of the mirror. She set her Judith Lieberman evening bag on the counter, flicking up the clasp on the beaded cowboy boot to retrieve her tube of lipstick, and then leaned in toward the mirror to assess her appearance. She looked flawless, of course, despite the lack of Chanel on her lips. "I saw you were seated at the table with Lara and Bryce Braddock. Any word from Ilsa and James? Are they enjoying their honeymoon?"

"Who wouldn't?" said Ainsley. "A handsome husband, a beautiful wife, a Mediterranean cruise? Why would they even want to come back?" Ainsley knew from her own phone conversations with Ilsa that the weeks had flown by, that the vacation was perfect, but that both were eager to come home and begin their life together at Braddock Hall. "I encouraged her to stay longer, but I imagine they'll be home next Thursday, as scheduled. Personally, I'd want my honeymoon to last as long as possible."

Miranda laughed. "I'm not sure you'd enjoy a two-week honeymoon, Ainsley. In fact, I'm not certain you'd make it a whole week away from Danfair. You're more of a homebody than anyone else I know."

And Ainsley, inexplicably, felt inadequate in a whole new area. Better to change the subject than try to defend her stay-at-home tendencies. Which didn't necessarily mean she wouldn't enjoy a long honeymoon. "Who were you sitting with at dinner?" she asked, as if she actually wanted to know.

"Carolyn, again." Miranda's lips formed a moue of vexation, but that could have had more to do with the faded lip color than with the seating arrangements. "I did meet someone you'd like, though. Peyton O'Reilly. Do you know who she is?"

Ainsley shook her head, watching her sister scroll up the lipstick.

"She's new to the area, just moved to Newport a couple of months ago. Her parents are the originators of the O'Reilly Diner chain of restaurants and they've just relocated the headquarters to Providence. Theirs is a real mom-and-pop success story." She touched the color to her lips. "Peyton is delightful and better yet, she's eager to volunteer. When I told her about

the new peds center, she practically begged to volunteer.'' Miranda pulled back from the mirror to observe, then leaned in again to dot the lipstick twice
more against her lower lip, twice more against her
upper, then finally, she pressed them together and
smoothed out the color. ''You look a little pale,'' she
said, glancing at Ainsley again, as she scrolled the
lipstick back down in the tube and recapped it. ''Is
something wrong with you?''

She was getting that question a lot lately. ''No,''
Ainsley sighed. Leaning in, she checked her cheeks
for color and thought she looked okay. Not as beautiful as her sister, who was wearing a gown of red
bandana-like fabric in keeping with the evening's
western theme and looked capable of stopping traffic
on the I-95 without half trying. Ainsley wondered, as
she often did, if she'd have preferred being beautiful
to being cute, but decided it wasn't a fair question
tonight. Not when Miranda had perfectly applied lipstick and she, herself, had none. She pursed her lips
at her reflection and, even before it occurred to her to
ask, Miranda offered the Chanel.

''I don't know why you won't carry a bag, Ainsley.
Then you'd have lipstick when you need it.''

''Oddly enough—'' she held up the tube as an example ''—I usually do have lipstick when I need it.''

''I meant, the right shade of lipstick,'' Miranda
said.

Ainsley applied and blotted. ''This is close

enough." She recapped the tube and handed it back to her sister. "Thank you."

"You're welcome. I haven't seen Bucky. Was he at your table?"

"Oh, yes." Ainsley had found Bucky to be quite annoying at dinner, although no one else had seemed to notice, so maybe it was just her mood. "I'm sure he's saving you a dance." Which made her think of Ivan. "Have you seen Ivan?" she asked with a return of enthusiasm. "He looks very handsome in his black denims and tuxedo jacket."

"Does he? I hadn't noticed," Miranda said, eyeing her sister in the mirror.

Of course not. That would be too easy. "Well, you should take another look. He's the best-looking man here."

Miranda dropped the tube of lipstick into her glittery little pod of an evening bag. "Ainsley, I have the strangest feeling you may be trying to set me up with Ivan."

Oops. "I don't know why you'd think that," she said, quickly on the defensive. "Are you *interested* in Ivan?"

Miranda studied her in the mirror for a long moment, then closed her bag with a pointed *snap*. "Frankly," she said. "I've never given it any thought."

Ainsley watched her sister walk out, newly lipsticked, gorgeous as always, the little pod purse swinging stylishly from her shoulder. Looking back at her own reflection, Ainsley realized the lipstick *was* the wrong shade for her.

Chapter Eight

"What's wrong with your lips?" Bucky asked the very second she returned to their table. "You look like you've been kissed hard by the sugarplum fairy."

Which didn't sound like a compliment. "I haven't been kissed by anyone for ages, but the right guy could remedy that."

"Oh, no, I'm not falling for that." He shook his head, obviously believing there was no question *he* was the right guy she referred to. "Then we'd both have that stuff on our lips. No thanks."

She sighed and sat down. "You're a true romantic, Bucky."

"You're not the first woman to tell me that," he said, sounding perfectly serious, and it crossed Ainsley's mind that she might have been too hasty in deserting Scott.

"Speaking of romantic," Bucky continued. "Let's dance. I believe they're playing our song."

She listened and decided "The Way You Look Tonight'' was romantic enough, considering her lips were sugarplum pink and therefore unkissable. She got up again and Bucky led her into the cluster of dancers, pulling her—with his usual deliberation— into his arms. With the ease of familiarity, she allowed Bucky to position her hands behind his neck, and her feet just naturally followed his lead into the rhythm of the dance. But then, over his shoulder, she caught a glimpse of Miranda's red dress as she sashayed by in the arms of the best-looking man at the gala. Ivan, no less.

Well, well, Ainsley thought, feeling an unsettling clutch of tension in her chest. She tried for a better look, but Bucky thwarted her efforts with a fancy turn and a series of complicated steps. He was the right height for her—five-ten to her five-five—but somehow tonight he seemed taller, as if he'd deliberately grown a couple of inches just to keep her from spying on her sister. Irritated, for no particular reason, she moved her head from side to side, trying to see around him.

''Is something wrong?'' he asked.

''No,'' she said, stopping her furtive glances. ''I'm fine. Perfectly fine.''

He nodded, taking her at her word. ''Your brother seems to be enjoying his evening out,'' Bucky observed. ''I'll admit I wasn't sure he would.''

Ainsley frowned at him. ''You were worried about Matt?''

He frowned back. "Why would I worry about Matt?"

Her eyes sought out her oldest brother, and her heart smiled at the sight of him. He looked every bit as handsome as Ivan did tonight and, bless his heart, he was sitting and talking animatedly with Julia Butterfield, a strapping and overly opinionated debutante who was, more often than not, a wallflower at these galas. Matt was kind, and Ainsley loved him for that. She worried about him, though, too. He was hard to read, but her instincts told her there was method behind his behavior and that by taking the noble course and spending much of the evening with the Julia Butterfields of society, he avoided the possibility of meeting someone special, someone he might fall in love with, someone who could offer him the real possibility of happily ever after.

"I wasn't worried about Matt," Bucky clarified.

"Well, Andrew isn't here, so naturally, I assumed…"

"I was talking about the doctor. Your *extra* brother. Remember him?"

"Ivan?"

"Of course, Ivan."

"I have no idea why you'd be worried about Ivan having a good time tonight. He always has a good time."

"I thought he might have a little trouble fitting in, that's all."

The dance came to a natural end, but she stood a moment and studied the man she'd become too accustomed to thinking she would marry some day. "You're an awful snob sometimes, Bucky, did you know that?"

"I am not a snob. I'm a realist. Big difference." His smile was slow and coaxing and, despite her efforts to be mad at him, rather persuasive. "You know what, Cuteness? Let's go outside and grab some fresh air, what do you say?"

"I don't think so," she said.

"Oh, come on," he wheedled. "You might get that kiss you were after."

For a second she thought about kissing him, outside, in the moonlight. But even from where she stood, she could tell the moon was hidden behind a bank of clouds and she knew in her heart Bucky's kiss would be no different than it always was. Pleasant, practiced, rather persuasive, with just the right amount of graduated pressure, just enough genuine desire to lure her in, bring up her expectations. But somehow—especially lately—she wound up feeling somehow dissatisfied after his kiss. As if he'd promised her Cloud Nine, but then decided she'd get dizzy if he took her higher than Cloud Five.

Ainsley sighed. Maybe she did know him too well, was too familiar with his moves. Maybe that's the way the best relationships worked. Maybe it was a good thing to be able to predict what her partner would do next in an embrace, where his hands would travel, when he'd part her lips with his tongue, how he'd smile at its conclusion. Until lately, she'd taken that knowledge as comfort, believed the familiarity was love. But just remembering the kiss she'd only imagined with Ivan brought a heated rush of color to her cheeks—so much for being pale!—and made her want to walk away from Bucky right now and not look back.

Which was stupid. Especially considering that imaginary kiss had been a hypothetical one between Ivan and Miranda and had nothing at all to do with her.

"Ainsley?" Bucky crooned, lifting a hand to his forehead as if he needed to shade his eyes. "Are you blushing? Or is that a reflection from those sugarplum lips?"

"I am *not* blushing," she said, although she could feel the sting of heat in her cheeks.

"Mmm-hmm…and I suppose you're *not* thinking about being kissed out in the moonlight, either."

"Not with these lips," she said irritably. "Besides, there isn't a moon. It's turning cloudy. I wouldn't be at all surprised if it rains buckets before the night is over."

"Then we'd better go outside now before it starts, don't you think?"

"No." She was tired of his smug teasing. "I'm not interested in going outside with you, Bucky."

He frowned, surprised and probably concerned by her unusual and—at least to him, anyway—completely illogical mood. ''Are you sure there's nothing wrong with you tonight?''

''Positive,'' she lied crisply. ''What could possibly be wrong with me?''

''Well, you're not dancing, for one thing.'' Ivan slipped up behind her and put his hands on her shoulders, drawing her away from Bucky by quick, subtle degrees. ''I'm going to steal your girl for a few minutes, Bucky. I hope you don't mind.''

Not waiting for a confirmation, or caring if one came, he turned her onto the dance floor and propelled her right to the center. ''You looked like you needed rescuing,'' he said, drawing her into his arms even before the next song began.

''I'm not his girl, you know.''

''He seems to believe you are.''

''Well, he's wrong.'' She knew, suddenly, and without reservation, that she wasn't going to marry Bucky. She didn't know why she'd ever thought she could. ''And what makes you think I couldn't save myself…if, as you say, I did need rescuing?''

''Instinct,'' he said. ''Pure, heroic instinct.''

Ainsley laughed, the first time since before dinner. ''Where have you been all night, Ivan? I've been drowning in a sea of solemnity. Practically everyone I've talked with at this gala has been so deadly *serious.*''

"You should have been at our table. We had a lot of laughs."

Because he'd been there, she knew. Because he dealt with serious stuff all the time and knew the wisdom of creating joy wherever he could. She'd always loved that about Ivan. He appreciated being able to laugh, was able to find humor and invite others to share it with him. "I wish I'd thought to switch place cards. Who was at your table?"

The music began, a pleasant melody that barely registered in Ainsley's thoughts as she found its rhythm, not so much dancing with Ivan as swaying with him in time.

"I didn't know there'd be a test. Let me see if I can remember all the names." He was quiet for a moment, apparently going around the table in his mind. "Let's see, on my right was Thea Braddock and next to her was her husband, Peter. He's the architect for the pediatric center, you know. Great guy. And I really liked Thea. She was on the quiet side, but radiant, if you know what I mean. She has a wonderful laugh."

Ainsley smiled, remembering Thea before she'd married Peter, grateful for the friendship she and Thea had built since then. "They're a wonderful couple, a true love match." It was on the tip of her tongue to tell him about her own part in bringing that match about, but remembered—just in time—that discretion was important. Especially as she was trying to work her way around to introducing Ivan to the possibility of a match with Miranda. Or at least, to laying the groundwork for it.

"And on your left?" she prompted.

"Julia Butterfield?" he suggested, as if he weren't sure he'd gotten the name correct. "A statuesque young lady, who told me a great deal about the difficulties in being a vegetarian."

"She's something of a health nut."

"But not much of a regular nut, apparently. Does she *have* a sense of humor?"

"It's hard to tell," Ainsley said. "I can't think of anyone who could say with certainty that she has a wonderful laugh."

"Maybe she's saving it for a really funny moment."

"Let's hope. Who was next to her?"

"Who was next to her," he repeated, his brow furrowing in concentration. "An older man. Nice-looking, with glasses. He *did* laugh, as I remember. Henry...McCarter." Ivan smiled, pleased with himself for remembering. "He's in banking. Then on the other side of him was a delightful little woman with tangerine hair and enough diamonds on her person to finance a small revolution. She kept the whole table in stitches, telling us about her various husbands. I think there may have been a dozen or so. The minute she discovered I wasn't married, she leaned right across the table and propositioned me. *Her* name I won't forget.''

"Lizzie Abrams," Ainsley announced confidently. "And I do hope you turned her down, Ivan, because besides being old enough to be your grandmother, she's way more woman than you can handle.''

He tried to look wounded by the remark. "Now, Ainsley, I believe you may be underestimating my experience with older women.''

"I've learned better than to underestimate Lizzie. Isn't she fabulous? She's the kind of woman I want to be when I'm eighty-four.''

"You don't have to wait, Ainsley. You could proposition thirty-four year-old men starting right now. As I didn't take Mrs. Abrams up on her generous offer, I'm still available.''

The laughter bubbled up in her throat. "I have other plans for you,'' she said, the words out before she quite realized how much they gave away.

He lifted his eyebrows. "Now that's an intriguing possibility.''

She gave him a blithely mysterious smile, as if she wasn't frantically trying to figure out a way to cover her tracks. "I think so, too.''

"Are you going to tell me your plans, or do I have to guess?''

"You'll never guess,'' she assured him.

"Ah, a challenge. Let's see…you need a burly hunk of man to move your furniture?''

"Move it where?"

"I don't know. That could be part of the plan."

"It could be, but it isn't, although I can see where you'd want to picture yourself as the burly hunk kind of furniture mover."

"I'll be happy to show you my muscles, if you have any doubts about that."

He was teasing, she knew, but the image of him, bare-chested and flexing his biceps for her inspection, brought a flush of heat to her cheeks again. "Tell me who you've danced with tonight," she said, swiftly changing the subject.

"Miranda. And you. But I'm still hoping to get to use my 'old football injury' before the night is over." He smiled and steered the conversation back. "Now, tell me about those plans."

"Can't," she said. "You'll just have to be patient."

"That's no fun. How about a clue? I'll make it easy for you—are these plans just for me or do they involve somebody else?"

She looked at him, lips pressed tightly together to make her point.

"Aha. I'm guessing these plans aren't just for me, are they, Miss Secret-Keeper? So…" He drew the word out, contemplating the possibilities. "Okay, I've got it—you're planning a part for me in the puppet show at the center's grand opening. That's the plan, isn't it?"

"Yes," she agreed readily. "I've written you in as Elton's straight man."

"I'll be good at that." The dance ended, but he showed no inclination to let her go. "But I don't think that's the plan we were talking about."

"Yes, it is," she replied, widening her eyes in feigned innocence. "It is."

"Oh, come on, Ainsley, you used to love guessing games. Remember that time you filled the Tiffany vase with jelly beans and made us all guess over and over again how many there were? Then when anybody got close, you changed the rules so we had to guess how many of each flavor there were."

She couldn't help but laugh. "Remember how Miranda kept saying she didn't even *like* jelly beans? And she accused you and Andrew of eating them to manipulate the count. But really she was just frustrated because I kept saying *'wrong!'* every time she made a guess."

"You did say it with rather obnoxious glee, as I recall. So, how many guesses do I get before you start bellowing out *'wrong!'*?"

She should have remembered how persistent he could be. "Guess away," she invited. "But I'm not giving you any hints like I did with the jelly beans."

"You gave me jelly beans, not hints." The band started another song, a zippy fast dance, and Ivan saw Bucky heading toward them, purpose written on his face. Grabbing Ainsley's hand, he pulled her with him toward the open terrace doors. "I could use a breath of fresh air. How about you?"

"Wait a minute, this isn't a version of that old football injury excuse, is it?"

"Nope, just a displaced Texan's need to see the sky." He kept hold of her hand, feeling brave and daring for luring her away from Bucky yet again. He didn't like that guy. Hadn't liked the way he'd been looking at Ainsley earlier. Or the condescending tone of his voice. Or the way he combed his hair, for that matter. Stepping onto the terrace with Ainsley in tow, Ivan kept moving quickly out into the balmy night. But the gardens were pleasantly lit for fresh-air-seeking guests and Ivan suddenly wanted more privacy. He didn't stop, but found and followed a wandering path through the flowering shrubs until they reached the lawn.

"The air's pretty fresh right here," she said, obviously wondering what he was doing, where he was leading her.

"Let's see how far we can walk before we fall into the Atlantic."

"That seems a little drastic."

"Why? Don't you feel like a swim?"

"What is this, Ivan, really? A last-ditch effort to avoid dancing with someone other than me?" She laughed.

The sound was as sweet in his ears as the distant

tumble of surf. "You forget, I've already danced with Miranda, too."

"And how was that?" Ainsley tried to sound disinterested, as if she really didn't care.

Ivan glanced at her, but kept moving, although he did slow the pace now that the night was deepening around them. "What do you mean, how was that? It was Miranda."

"Exactly."

Stopping, he turned to face her. "And what does 'exactly' mean?"

She looked almost startled at the question, then offered a teasing shrug. "Nothing," she said. "What else is there to say about my sister except *exactly?*"

But he knew every tone in her voice, every nuance of her face, and he recognized her expression for what it was. A caught-in-the-act look if he'd ever seen one. And he'd seen enough to know she was now trying to back-pedal her way out of a conversation she wished she hadn't started. "I'd say, you've summed it up nicely." He let her off the hook for the moment, but only because he wanted a minute or two to think about what, *exactly,* she was up to.

And what he thought she was up to was matchmaking.

"Miranda is pretty great," he offered up as a test of his theory. "I'd say she's exactly perfect."

Ainsley hesitated for a moment, as if taken aback.

"I don't know that I'd say she was *perfect*, exactly, but then she is *my* sister."

The stress on the possessive was pointed and the underlying meaning hard to miss. Which was that Miranda wasn't *his* sister. "I'm surprised she hasn't been swept off her feet by some lucky fella," he said, leading her on.

"I know," she agreed eagerly. Too eagerly. "It's almost as much of a mystery as why some pretty great female hasn't nabbed you."

"Don't forget I was propositioned just a little while ago."

She laughed easily, probably believing she was making progress with her plans. "Lizzie—" she said with feigned consideration "—would be more than a match for you, I'm afraid, Ivan. I think you need to look for someone a little younger and perhaps not so worldly wise."

"I suppose you're right. Do you think Miranda...?" It was as close to trapping her as he could get without flat out asking the question.

The silence stretched, and he could almost sense Ainsley's racing thoughts. "Miranda?" Her voice came out pitched with surprise, as if the idea had never occurred to her. "I can't say I ever thought about you and Miranda like that."

Bingo. "Can't say I ever have either," he said. "Which is a good thing since she told me not five minutes ago that she's involved with some guy."

"She is?" The words practically exploded out of Ainsley's mouth. "She told you that?"

He lifted his shoulders in a shrug that could have meant anything. It was a lie, of course, but he felt Ainsley deserved a little hitch in her getalong for plotting his future behind his back.

"Who is he? Why don't I know about him? When did she have time to meet…" The questions dwindled away as logic caught up with her. "Miranda didn't mention another guy," she said, with a wry look. "She wouldn't admit that, even if it were true."

He shook his head, the corners of his mouth lifting in a *gotcha* kind of smile. "Matt told me about the connections you make at IF Enterprises, that it's a matchmaking business."

She sighed. "Well, it's not a complete secret. I just try not to blab it to everyone I meet."

"I didn't think you considered me *everyone*." He didn't want to make her feel guilty, though. He simply wanted to set the record straight about one match she wasn't going to make. "It would never work with Miranda," he said. "We're too different."

"But that's exactly why it will work. Opposites attract. They complement each other."

He was tempted to laugh, because she was so passionately wrong. "There's more to it than that, Ainsley."

She drew herself up. "I'm the matchmaker," she said. "I think I know what I'm talking about."

It was not the sort of thing he wanted to argue. She was struggling to find herself in this family of over-achievers. They'd protected her, sheltered her, made her feel she had to fight for their respect...and she was finally making strides toward finding her true identity. He wanted to encourage her, not shake her new confidence. Even if he was certain—in this case, anyway—that she didn't have a clue what she was talking about. "You're right, Ainsley. I apologize. You have great insight into what makes people tick and you're a heck of a lot better at reading people than anyone else I know. I have no doubts you're a wonderful matchmaker." He gave a smile to affirm that belief, as well as to soften the coming qualifica-tion. "It's just that I can't see anything happening between Miranda and me. I'm fairly certain she'd be horrified at the prospect."

"Well, I wasn't going to *tell* her," Ainsley said, and then released a long sigh. "Of course, I didn't mean to tip my hand with you, either. I'm not very good at this, Ivan. First Scott and now this. I may as well resign before Ilsa fires me."

"That doesn't sound like a *Lizzie* kind of attitude. Besides, Matt told me that Mrs. Fairchild had ample opportunities to take on an apprentice before you came along, but you're the first she's accepted. He's really proud of the way you went after the position."

"He is?" The sparkle reappeared in her eyes.

"He did," Ivan confirmed truthfully, wishing Matt

had told her himself, wishing all of her siblings could give her credit for the many talents she possessed. "And what's more, Miranda and I aren't clients. We're more of a…test case. No one's even going to know it didn't work out, unless you tell them."

Her eyebrows rose in a confident arch, and he fell in love with her resilient spirit all over again. "It could work out if you'd only look at the possibilities, Ivan. Don't be so closed to the idea that something *might* happen if you gave it a chance."

Having just spent the length of "The Way You Look Tonight" dancing with Miranda, he knew nothing was going to happen. If there'd ever been that possibility with Miranda, it had faded a long time ago. She wasn't interested in him except as a friend, and the crush he'd once had on her had fizzled out long ago. There was nothing there to open himself to, no latent attraction to build on, no spark to fan into flame.

But there was a spark with Ainsley.

The truth was suddenly, unexpectedly there, shifting, tumbling, turning itself inside out and becoming a certainty in his heart even before his head completed the leap. It was *Ainsley* who held the possibilities for him. *Ainsley,* who had always fascinated and continually surprised him. *Ainsley,* who had grown up while he'd been away and become the woman he wanted to share his life with.

He was in love with Ainsley.

The idea was new and yet, somehow, it must have been in his heart forever. It scared him, excited him, made him feel hopeful and confused and uncertain of what to do about it. This could be trouble. She still regarded him as her *extra* brother and he wasn't sure how to begin to change her perception. Or even if he should. Her parents might think he wasn't a suitable match for her, either. Matt might object. He hadn't seemed to mind when they'd talked about Miranda. But this was Ainsley. The baby of the family. The one they were so protective of. Lord knew, he couldn't offer her anything like the lifestyle she already had. In choosing to work for the Foundation, he'd forfeited much of the income he might have made in private practice. But Ainsley wouldn't care about that, even if her family might. No, of course they wouldn't, either. They were generous people to whom class mattered less than character...and they'd given him a position within the Foundation, showed their confidence in him by making him a part of their mission. They wouldn't object. Well, he didn't think they would.

But he was jumping too far ahead, planning for a life with Ainsley when he didn't even know how to set about convincing her he was not her brother, *extra* or otherwise.

"You're thinking about it, aren't you?" she asked, a pleased smile curving her lips. Lips that he wished to kiss with such instant hunger it made his mouth uncomfortably dry. "You're considering the possibilities."

"Yes," he said in a voice that sounded hoarse and needy. He needed time to think, to plan, so he did the only thing that occurred to him...he cleared his throat. "We'd better go back," he said, turning toward the house and enough light to either dispel his revelation...or confirm it. "I think it's going to rain."

She hung back. "This from the guy who was ready to go for a swim not two minutes ago?"

"It doesn't seem like a prudent thing to do all of a sudden."

Her giggle teased him. "If Lizzie heard that, she'd withdraw her proposition immediately. Come on, Ivan, stay with me. I'm not ready to go back in just yet."

He couldn't very well protest that they *had* to return to the ballroom. "Why?" he asked. "Are you hoping to get wet?"

"That would be one way of avoiding Bucky," she said, as if considering her options. "But since he brought me to this dance, I suppose I'll have to let him take me home."

Over my dead body. "I'll take you home."

"Are you trying to rescue me again?"

Her smile was as familiar to him as a sunset in the hill country of Texas, but it seemed suddenly, dangerously, sexy. "No, ma'am," he said. "I know you're perfectly capable of rescuing yourself if you want to.''

''Damn straight,'' she said with a laugh, and he wondered how she could be so unaware of his change of heart when it was all he could do to keep from pulling her into his arms right now and demonstrating how he felt with a kiss. Which would be the best way to ruin their friendship and any chance she'd ever look at him differently. ''I'm not going to marry Bucky,'' she said out of the blue. ''I decided tonight when he said he wouldn't kiss me.''

''The man is clearly an idiot,'' Ivan said before he could stop himself.

She laughed again, which assured him her heart wasn't broken. ''Tell me something, Ivan. Do you think I'm kissable?''

His heart jumped at the question, but he forced himself to consider who she thought she was asking. ''Well, now, that's a hard question for me to answer.''

''You're not my brother,'' she said sternly. ''So don't think you can get out of answering with that excuse. You're a man. And I want a man's opinion. If you wanted to kiss me, would the color of my lipstick stop you?''

He paused, half-expecting a punchline. But she simply looked up at him, her attitude firmly in place, so he handed her an honest answer. ''If I wanted to kiss you, Ainsley, nothing would stop me.''

She blinked, as if she'd heard the conviction in his voice, as if she could feel the heat of desire burning a hole in his self-control. "Oh," she said. "Oh."

"Ainsley?" It was Bucky's voice, coming from the terrace, unwittingly rescuing Ivan from what would have proved a terrible mistake.

"Ssshhh…." Ainsley stepped closer, her body nudging him to secrecy. "It's Bucky. Hide me."

They were standing in the shadows of the night, but otherwise in plain view on the lawn. "He's bound to see us," Ivan whispered. "Your dress doesn't exactly blend in."

She frowned up at him. "Think of something, then," she said. "I'm in a great mood now and I don't want him to spoil it yet."

Ivan felt a swirl of pleasure, whether at the idea that he was the cause of her great mood or because of her nearness. Either one seemed enough cause to be happy. "Does this mean you *want* me to rescue you?" he asked in a teasing undertone.

"Oh, for Pete's sake," she said…and going up on her tiptoes, she pulled his head down to hers and kissed him.

Surprise kept him immobile for a second. But only one. The timing was too close to his discovery to allow for resistance, his desire too new to be reined in. So he folded her into his arms and welcomed the feel of her soft lips pressing insistently on his…and tried to keep his heart from betraying him with its arrhythmic beating beneath her palm.

"Ainsley?" Bucky called again, louder this time, closer.

But Ivan wasn't ready for this first sweet taste of love to end and he caught her close, shifting so that she was shielded from sight by his body. He felt surprise ripple through her, sensed a startled awareness in her response. He knew he should be careful, but the feel of her in his arms, beneath his kiss, was powerful and new and he was having trouble keeping even this tight a rein on his actions. Kissing her like this, carefully, holding his emotions in check, telling himself to pull away before he lost what semblance of control he still had, was agony. But it would be so much worse to get totally lost in the moment and lose any hope of the future.

Before he could bring the decision into action, she jerked back, suddenly, startling him with the ferocity of her alarm. Pressing a hand to her mouth, she looked at him with eyes widened by confusion and an expression he couldn't, didn't want to, name. "Oh," she gasped. "Oh, no. I'm…I'm sorry, Ivan. I'm so sorry!" And then she was running across the lawn, away from him.

Ivan followed her progress through the garden, tracing her movements by the shimmer of reflected light off her beaded gown. He had no trouble at all seeing her run, beneath the lights of the garden, up to the edge of the terrace and straight into Bucky's arms. He watched, like a deer caught in the headlights, as she lifted her face and Bucky bent toward her, obviously no longer averse to kissing her so kissable lips.

Closing his eyes, Ivan turned his back to the disturbing scene, tuned out the music and tried to hear only the surf pounding against the cliffs. Even when the rain started to fall in warm, fat drops, he stood there, wondering how to return to the moment when he'd realized he was in love with Ainsley and before he'd ruined everything by taking advantage of her impulsive kiss. He knew how impulsive she could be, understood she'd meant the kiss as a sham, as a way of hiding from someone she didn't want to see her. He'd known that the moment it happened, and yet he'd turned the kiss into a declaration, drawn a line in the sand that couldn't be crossed.

The rain continued, soaking into his clothes, stinging him with the sure knowledge that in one unguarded moment he'd wiped away more possibilities than he'd ever imagined possible.

Chapter Nine

Ainsley tucked the files she was carrying into the crook of her arm and was preparing to knock on Ilsa's office door when it opened. She found herself chin to chest with Ivan.

"Hello, Ainsley," he said, his voice and expression revealing less surprise than resignation at seeing her there.

"Oh," she gasped, giving away in one word exactly how very startled she was to see him. "Hello." Her gaze darted past him to Ilsa, who was standing just back from the doorway as if she'd been seeing him out. Being a lady to her marrow, Ilsa always saw her guests to the door. It was a small gesture, but one she assured Ainsley was worth the effort in helping clients feel comfortable with their decision to solicit a matchmaker's services.

Bringing her gaze back to Ivan, Ainsley wondered what he was doing here. To say he was the last person she'd expected to run into coming out of Ilsa's office was an understatement. She hadn't seen him in over two weeks, had studiously avoided any chance encounter. And, as it hadn't been particularly difficult, she'd reluctantly concluded he was avoiding her, too. But suddenly, here they were, face-to-face, and there was nothing to do but pretend they hadn't both been hoping to avoid an awkward moment like this, indefinitely.

"I didn't expect to see you here," she said.

"I was just about to stop by your office," he said at the same time, their words colliding, their self-consciousness equal and obvious.

"You w-were?" She stammered a little, certain somehow that he'd hoped not to see her at all.

"I wouldn't miss a chance to see that view." There was a smile in his voice but not in his eyes, and she felt another hard knot of sorrow form in her throat. She'd missed him something awful, but worse than that, she kept reliving the moment on the lawn at Rosecliff when she'd seen the dismay, the horror, in his eyes. She'd ruined their friendship with one silly, impulsive act, without an ounce of forethought to the consequences, and if she'd had any doubt before, she could see now that there was no way to fix it. No matter how great her regret.

"It's still a great view," she said, hardly aware of what she was saying. "I've been so busy, I haven't had much time to appreciate it these past two weeks." She wanted to bite her tongue at being so specific, at pinning her sudden busyness to the two weeks since the Denim & Diamonds gala. "I guess you've been pretty busy yourself. The center opens Sunday, huh?"

"Come rain or shine." He nodded and there they stood, in the doorway of Ilsa's office, caught in a clumsy, uncomfortable, awkward situation. "I suppose I'll see you there."

"Wouldn't miss it." Although she was wishing now that she might.

Ivan glanced over his shoulder at Ilsa, and when he looked back at Ainsley her curiosity peaked. What *was* he doing here?

"I guess I should be going," he said as if he wasn't already halfway out the door. "Thanks again, Mrs. Braddock," he said. "I'll look forward to working with you on that...project."

Project? Ainsley couldn't help it. She had to know why he was here. "Project?" she asked. "You two are working on a project?"

Ilsa's eyebrows went up, but Ivan merely smiled. As he would at a child's inappropriate question. "She's agreed to co-chair a benefit for the center," he said. "Next spring."

"Oh." She looked past him to where Ilsa stood, smiling. Of course, Ilsa really hadn't *stopped* smiling since she'd returned from her honeymoon. "That's nice of you."

"I'm happy to have been asked to help," Ilsa said. "It'll be fun."

"Fun." Ainsley nodded. "That's good, then. Fun is good." And *she* was an idiot, which she'd proven beyond a doubt when she'd kissed Ivan. *Really* kissed him. Not some soft, affectionate bussing that could be construed as an expression of friendship. Not a mere brushing of lips against lips that might be explained away as fondness. Oh, no. It had been a genuine *rock-my-world* kiss. Even now, the memory burned her and she fought down a blush with sheer force of will.

"Maybe I'll take a rain check on that view," Ivan suggested, as if her remembering the kiss had made him remember it, too, and caused him to think twice about the wisdom of being alone with her. In her office or anywhere else. "I should get back out to the center. Staff meetings this afternoon."

Ainsley's head bobbed agreement. "Can't be late for staff meetings," she said, as if she'd know.

"Goodbye, Mrs. Braddock. I'll get you that information as soon as possible." His smile was warm with gratitude and genuine appreciation, but faded as it flickered back to Ainsley. "Goodbye, Ainsley."

He stepped out, brushing casually against her as he passed, showing not a single sign that he wanted to hear anything she had to say. Not even goodbye.

She watched him go, wanting to run after him, apologize, say anything to put things back the way they'd been before. But everything had changed in the moment she'd kissed him. Between one heartbeat and the next, she'd discovered what she wanted…and made certain she could never have it. Ivan thought of her as a friend, as his little sister, and he was embarrassed by the passion that kiss had aroused in her and that she'd displayed with such abandon. Knowing him as she did, she suspected he was almost as embarrassed by his having let it happen as he was by her action in initiating it. But then, what choice had she given him? It wasn't like she'd explained that she needed him to kiss her as a ruse to get rid of the unwanted Bucky. Oh, no, she'd just puckered up and kissed him. She'd done it impulsively, thinking only that Bucky wouldn't intrude on a private moment, not really *thinking* at all, and now she couldn't go back and undo what she'd done. She'd ruined everything in a split second and her relationship with Ivan would never be the same, no matter how many times she said she was sorry.

"Ainsley?" Ilsa said. "Are you all right?"

Forcing a false brightness onto her face, into her voice, she turned toward the older woman. "Of course," she said. "What could possibly be wrong with me?"

"…AND WE'RE PROUD today to dedicate The Jonathan Danville Children's Research Center to the children of the world." Charles Danville moved away from the microphone to help Linney manipulate the oversize scissors and cut the wide yellow ribbon, officially opening the new facility.

Ainsley applauded along with the crowd. It felt good to be a Danville today. The center was a long-held dream of her mother's, a concept the Foundation's trustees had been working on for most of the last decade. And now it was a reality. It would offer medical treatment to children with neuromuscular diseases and defects, regardless of their ability to pay. And it would provide hope for the future through research that would be shared freely with other scientists and doctors around the globe. It was a proud day for the Foundation. A proud day for Charles and Linney Danville.

Having her parents home for the opening was a special treat, and Ainsley was glad they'd be spending the rest of the week at Danfair. They wouldn't stay long. They never did. But anytime they were home was a joyous, almost giddy occasion. It had been that way for as long as she could remember. Life at Danfair with her brothers and sister and a rotating staff of caregivers was happy enough, but when Charles and Linney came home, it was Christmas and birthdays and every other exhilarating occasion all rolled into one. And it lasted until they left again. Which they always did…sooner rather than later.

But Ainsley had learned not to think about the leaving or how much she'd miss them when they were gone. What mattered was the time they had and that it remained free of discord. Over the years, neither she nor any of her siblings had wanted to diminish their parents' joy in coming home, not by even a moment. So they'd kept the little issues, the little heartaches, to themselves, choosing not to sully the small amounts of time they had together as a normal family.

Which was why Ainsley was making more effort than usual to be her bright, bubbly, carefree, and *not* serious self. This was a truly special time for her family and she wasn't going to spoil it by letting anyone see that she was suffering. Especially since she was singly and solely responsible for her own misery.

Even had she been inclined to share, she wasn't sure she could bear her mother's assurances that a little heartache would keep her sensitive. Nor did she want to hear her father remind her of all the problems she didn't have to face. She didn't want Matt patting her shoulder sympathetically. She didn't want Miranda telling her what she should have done, what she still should do. She didn't even want a comforting hug from Andrew, who could have come closest to actually making her feel better. Unless she counted Ivan, who had always been able to show her a silver lining, no matter how gloomy her mood.

But she couldn't turn to Ivan this time. Thanks to her lack of forethought, discretion and simple common sense. She didn't know what she'd do to ease the awkwardness she'd introduced into their relationship, didn't know if there was anything she *could* do. But she knew, eventually, she'd have to try.

Just not today.

Today was a day to praise and support this new example of Danville philanthropy. The children's research center was her parents' dream, that was true, but she understood what it meant to Ivan, as well. He'd worked all of his life for this, would devote the rest of his life and every ounce of determination he had to making it a success, and she wasn't about to do anything to lessen his pride and happiness in this moment of beginning.

The line of VIPs was moving through the front doors now and into the lobby, where the reception was to be held. The guests began to follow, bunching up in front of the building. Ainsley hung back, letting the crowd fold in around her. She didn't want to be inside with the family just yet, didn't want to shake hands and be congratulated. Chances are, in all the hubbub, she wouldn't even be missed.

"Ainsley! Ainsley, wait for me!"

She stopped, looked behind her and, with sinking spirits, saw her cousin, Scott, snaking his way through the crowd toward her.

"Hi, thanks, I need to talk to you," he said in one breath.

"Great." She tried to look happy about it, too. She didn't want to talk to him. Not really. Not again. But she at least owed him a sympathetic ear. "Let's go in and get some punch and then we'll talk, okay?"

He seemed agreeable with that, perhaps largely because, as they jostled their way through the doorway, there wasn't much opportunity to talk. Scott didn't hesitate, though, once they were inside. He walked straight over, got her a cup of sherbet punch, brought it back to her and, before she could raise the cup to her lips, blurted out, "There was never anything between Molly and that guy at The Torrid Tomato."

"Hmm," she said. "That's good."

He nodded. "I was hoping you'd think so." And he launched into a rambling account of how he'd managed to uncover this information.

Ainsley listened distractedly as she looked around the room, telling herself she was *not* looking for Ivan, even though she stopped looking the moment her gaze found him. He was in a dark suit, which made him seem somehow stern and very seriously handsome. But then he smiled, and her heart felt the humor that was so much a part of him. He shook hands with one of the trustees and then turned to speak to Charles Danville, sharing a laugh, acknowledging an introduction. Matt joined them for a moment, and when her father drifted off with an old friend, Miranda took his place.

Ainsley watched from across the room as Ivan's head bent to capture whatever words Miranda was speaking to him. Her heart ached a little, wishing she could be there, too, in the middle of their conversation instead of caught in the looping, convoluted chronicle of Scott's investigations. But even if she'd been right beside Ivan, she knew she wouldn't have been a part of it. Not really. If she'd been there, his conversation would have been less intimate, more restrained, no longer open and unreservedly honest.

Her feelings for Ivan had changed and he knew it. The easy camaraderie they'd had as close friends couldn't surmount the uneasy tensions of unrequited love. And she *was* in love with Ivan, who thought of her merely as a little sister. She wasn't even certain he considered her a grown-up. All of which meant she'd have to get used to being on the outside of conversations between Ivan and the members of her family. Over time, maybe he'd stop feeling betrayed. Over time, maybe she'd stop yearning for the way things had been. With enough time, maybe they'd reclaim a measure of the ease she'd once taken so for granted.

Miranda laughed suddenly, unexpectedly, causing her beauty to shine through warmly and vibrantly, and when she placed her hand on Ivan's forearm in an intimate, confiding gesture, Ainsley felt a physical ache around her heart. She'd wanted to make a match between her sister and Ivan, and apparently the seeds she'd sown—however indiscreetly—had taken root. Miranda might never have thought about Ivan as a possible match, but once the idea was in her mind, it seemed as if she just couldn't ignore it. And from the look on Ivan's face as he smiled down at her, he had obviously reconsidered his opinion of the possibilities as well.

How fittingly ironic, Ainsley thought, that this would be the match she'd actually gotten right.

"So," Scott concluded. "What do you think?"

She thought she wanted to go home. "It's what you think that counts," she said truthfully, if a little vaguely.

"But I want your advice, Ainsley. I need your opinion as a matchmaker. What should I do about Molly?"

"Whatever your heart tells you," she said, because really, what did she know? It might actually work for him. "Be brave for once, Scott. Do what you want to do."

"Dad won't like it. No one in the family will."

She lifted her eyebrow, challenged him to step out and change his life, if that's what he wanted. "Is that more important to you than Molly?"

He seemed to get taller, right before her eyes. "You're right. What's important is how I feel about Molly."

She offered him the best smile she could manage and hoped he'd take it for encouragement. She still believed he and Molly were a bad idea. She still believed he'd have found a better match in Shelby Stewart. But Ilsa was right. Her job as a matchmaker was to introduce the possibilities and then step back and see what happened.

"Thanks, Ainsley." Scott pumped her hand excitedly. "You're a terrific matchmaker. I mean it. Really terrific."

Her gaze slipped sadly back to Ivan and Miranda. She *was* a terrific matchmaker, she thought with a sigh. A really terrific matchmaker.

IVAN FELT her gaze on him, and it was all he could do to pretend he was unaware. He knew if he looked over at her, her glance would skitter away, as if she hadn't been looking at him at all. He knew if he approached her, she'd find a hasty reason to be somewhere else. He knew if he tried to apologize, it would only embarrass her…and make him feel worse. If that was possible.

Ilsa had advised him to be patient, to give Ainsley time to sort out her emotions, to stay away from her as much as possible. He hated the pretense, missed her like crazy, but what good was there in obtaining the services of an excellent matchmaker if he didn't follow her advice?

And the answer, of course, was none.

He'd messed up his relationship with Ainsley and didn't know how to put it right again. Or if there was even any chance it could be right again. He was in love with a woman who considered him the next best thing to her big brother. If there'd ever been much chance she would see him in a different light, he'd scrubbed that future with one impulsive, passionate embrace.

But Ilsa had assured him she would help. She said she'd noticed a spark and thought he and Ainsley might be a match the first time she'd seen them together. She had good instincts for possibilities, she'd told him. He needed to trust her judgment and stay away from Ainsley until the moment for an *introduction of possibilities* came along.

But that moment would not come today.

"My family does throw the best parties," Miranda said confidently from beside him. "Even if I do say so myself."

"You'll get no argument from me." Ivan smiled at her. "Of course, before I met Matt, the only parties I'd ever been to featured birthday cake, party whistles and a whoopee cushion."

She laughed, unexpectedly, with a throaty pleasure that made him wonder why she did it so seldom. "You've come a long way, Ivan," she said.

It was true. He was light-years away from the little frame house in west Texas where he'd first dreamed of serving in a facility like this one. A long, long way from the day he'd promised Emma that he'd spend his life helping children like her. "I can't tell you how glad I am to be here, Miranda. Or how fortunate I feel to have a part in this."

"We're fortunate you're crazy enough to want to

be a part of it, Ivan. Believe it or not, there aren't that many we would trust with this endeavor. It takes a special commitment and a great deal of personal sacrifice to make the world a better place. We might have searched for years and never found anyone as gifted and dedicated as you.'' She put her hand on his arm and leaned closer to confide, ''Plus, it's always nice when the perfect candidate is a close, personal friend.''

''That might make it more difficult to maintain a business relationship, you know.''

She shook her head, smiling. ''Not when the business is the Foundation. Somehow, the common goal of philanthropy seems to smooth out those differences.'' She paused, the smile fading. ''But speaking of differences, there is one thing I wanted to talk to you about. This probably isn't the best time, but...well, I didn't know if you were aware that Ainsley is working as a...'' Miranda stopped, as if she was hesitant to reveal the secret, or maybe a little embarrassed.

''...matchmaker,'' Ivan said, saving her the trouble of saying it aloud. ''I know. Matt told me.''

Miranda looked relieved. ''She's only an apprentice and I imagine she'll have decided to pursue some other...career...before she manages to do any real harm in this one. But I thought I should warn you that she's trying to get us together.''

''Us?'' Ivan asked, although of course he knew.

"You know what I mean."

"Yes, actually, I do."

"So she spilled the beans to you, too." Miranda shook her head and came close to rolling her eyes.

"She thinks we'd make a perfect match."

Miranda regarded him for a moment, as if unsure how to proceed. "I hope you don't agree with her, Ivan, because I'm afraid she's very much mistaken about that."

Ivan wanted to defend Ainsley, wanted to stand up for her right to be a success, wanted her to have the respect of this sister she so admired, but he also wanted to be straight with Miranda. "I imagine apprentices in every line of work make mistakes."

"Which I hope means you're not upset that I'm...well, not interested in that kind of relationship with you."

He couldn't help but smile. "I'm not heartbroken, no. I was fairly certain you'd feel that way. I even told Ainsley as much."

"She came right out and talked to you about this?"

"I guessed," he admitted. "She tried to convince me to consider the possibilities."

Miranda sighed. "She was pretty obvious about it. Sometimes I wonder if she's ever going to grow up and stop being so impulsive."

Now, he felt he could rightfully defend her. "She has grown up, Miranda. But she isn't like you. She's never going to do things the way you do them or see life the way you see it. She may always be a little impulsive and she may never completely conquer her tendency to speak first and think better of it afterward. Which only means we need to celebrate who she is, and not focus on what she isn't.''

Miranda looked surprised, if not entirely convinced. ''You know, Ivan, you and Ainsley have a lot in common. Has that ever occurred to you?''

''Maybe,'' he answered, trying to give little, if anything, away.

She nodded, a half smile curving her lips. ''You might want to consider the possibility,'' she said.

''Possibility of what?'' Matt asked, coming up just in time to hear his sister's last comment.

''The world is full of possibilities, Matthew,'' Miranda said. ''I would have thought you'd know that.'' She moved off, greeting someone else, leaving Ivan to explain, if he cared to.

''Women are more trouble than they're worth,'' Matt stated flatly. ''And sisters are the worst of the lot.''

''I never thought your sisters were all that bad.'' Ivan slipped a hand into his pocket, nodded to one of the doctors on the center's advisory board. ''And since my own sister was sick from the day she was born, I'm not sure I know how aggravating she might have been under different circumstances.''

''I'm sorry, Ivan. That was a thoughtless thing for me to say. And you know I'm crazy about my sisters.

It's just lately—the past two weeks, really—they've been getting on my nerves.''

Ivan laughed. ''Everything's been getting on your nerves lately. I think that's called, 'opening-day jitters.' ''

''Maybe so. I just know Miranda's been so bossy, even Andrew has threatened to send her off with Mother and Dad when they leave. And believe me, they don't want her with them, either.''

''What about Ainsley?'' Ivan asked. He didn't think she would have told anyone about the kiss, but he wasn't positive she hadn't. ''What's she done to drive you nuts?''

''Oh, nothing really. She's just been moping around, not listless, exactly, but not herself, either. I suppose it's because she broke her engagement to Bucky. She's been dating him a long time.''

''They weren't engaged,'' Ivan said, a little more emphatically than he'd intended. ''She told me they weren't.''

Matt shrugged. ''Maybe not, but they gave a good imitation of a couple who were planning a future together. I never thought he made her all that happy, but then I'm just her big brother. What do I know?''

''What kind of guy do you think would make her happy, Matt?''

Looking across the room at his baby sister, Matt's expression went softly thoughtful. ''That's not an easy question for a brother to answer,'' he said. ''But just between you and me? I always sort of hoped she'd choose someone like you.''

''Me?''

''Well, you don't think I'd choose a boring guy like Bucky for a brother-in-law, do you?'' Matt grinned and clapped Ivan on the back. ''It'd be nice to have my sisters pick somebody I actually like.''

Ivan returned the grin, with a lighter heart than he'd had only minutes ago. ''You should be careful what you wish for, Danville,'' he warned. ''You never know but that you might get it.''

Across the room, Ainsley saw her brother thump Ivan's elbow with his own, watched as Ivan bumped back. It was a confusing bit of male horseplay she'd seen them do many times before, the way they said, *'Hey, that's great,'* to each other without really saying anything at all. A less obvious *'Good play, buddy'* than a slap on the butt. It was no wonder, she thought, that women didn't understand men.

Andrew came up beside her, holding a drink in each hand. ''I'm looking for a red dress,'' he said.

''Good luck,'' she answered.

He frowned at her. ''I can't believe it. I give you the best straight line you're likely to hear all day and you can't come up with anything better than *good luck?*''

''What did you expect me to say?''

''Oh, how about, *'Red will clash with your hair, Andrew. Try a nice blue or green, instead.'* You know, you seem to have lost your sense of humor lately. Even your smile doesn't seem very happy.''

And she'd thought she was doing such a good job of putting on a happy face. ''This is a solemn occasion,'' she said in self-defense.

He handed her one of the drinks. ''Here, you need this more than Marielle.''

''Who's Marielle?''

''My date for this auspicious occasion. Want to meet her?''

Ainsley shook her head. ''I don't think so. You keep your photography assistants around longer than you do the women you date. Oh, I forgot to ask before. How did Hayley do on her own while you were in Salt Lake City?''

''Beautifully,'' he answered. ''I don't think I've ever come back to find the studio in better shape. So apparently, it's only my presence that makes her break things. She still jumps a foot any time I walk into the room, but she doesn't squeak as much.'' He took a sip of his drink. ''Ivan looks like he's really enjoying himself. Anything ever come of that idea you had that he and Miranda would make a good match?''

A lump the size of New Hampshire rose in Ainsley's throat. ''Maybe,'' she said as brightly as possible. ''These things take time.''

''The best things usually do.'' He tapped his glass against hers. ''Here's to you, Ainsley, the apprentice matchmaker," he said. "May you always get it right." He drank to her, then scanned the crowd. "If you see a pretty blonde in a red dress, send her my way."

And he was gone, replaced almost immediately by Bucky.

"Hello, Cuteness."

Great. Just what she needed. Buckingham Ellis Winston, IV. "Hello, Bucky," she said coolly and took a sip of the punch.

"I've been looking for you. Thought maybe you'd be ready to talk to me now."

She turned toward him as she lowered the punch glass, not wanting to be rude, but not wanting to go over the same ground again, either. "I believe we've already said all there is to say, Bucky. What is there left to talk about?"

Wrong question. Wrong, wrong, wrong. To someone like Bucky, who was seldom at a loss for words, it was the exact wrong thing to say.

"I thought you'd be over your snit by now," he began. "I thought you'd be ready to listen to reason."

"I'm not going to marry you, Bucky. Please, let's not have this conversation. Not here. Not today."

"If you'd take my phone calls or agree to go to dinner one evening, it wouldn't have to be here, today. But I'm getting to the end of my rope here. You're going to have to talk to me sooner or later."

With a soft, determined sigh, she shook her head.

"This is a special day for my family and the Foundation," she said. "Let's save our personal drama for a more appropriate place and time."

"I think this is the perfect place," he said stubbornly. "We can just step back into one of the offices and talk about this. No one will even know we're not out here mingling with the crowd."

"No. The Foundation is important to me and I'm not going to leave the reception for this wonderful new medical facility to listen to you tell me what a mistake I'm making."

He smiled. "The Foundation's important to me, too, Ainsley, but not as important as you. Come on, Cuteness, let's get this settled."

It was true. She knew she *was* more important to him than the work of the Foundation, than this children's center, than probably anything else in his life. He'd always, right from the start, put her first. Had that been the attraction? Had *that* been the reason she'd thought she could marry him? *Should* marry him?

Bucky had worked for the Foundation all the time they'd been dating, and it had never once crossed her mind to wonder when he would become lost in the cause, sucked into a life of ceaseless sacrifice. She'd known he'd be home on time, at dinner every evening, never out trying to make the world a better place, never making any sacrifice that cost him—or her—a moment's discomfort. In that way, he'd seemed safe, but now, suddenly, she thought he was simply pointless. "Okay," she said slowly. "Since you insist, we'll do this right here, right now. For the last time, Bucky, it's over. Don't call me. Don't drop by. Don't send flowers. Don't arrange any accidental meetings. And whatever you do, don't ever call me *Cuteness,* again."

He blinked and opened his mouth, but she lifted a finger to shush him…and strangely enough, Bucky complied.

At least long enough for her to turn and walk away from him for the last time. Her spirits lifted with every step, the corners of her mouth rose, too. That had felt good. Really good.

This was a good day to be a Danville…even one with a slightly broken heart.

Chapter Ten

Ainsley didn't know why Ilsa had given her this assignment.

"This research has to be done without anyone—and I do mean, anyone—suspecting what you're doing," Ilsa had said. *"Discretion is the most important part of the assignment, Ainsley. I cannot stress that enough."*

Ainsley had gotten the picture. Keep her mouth shut. Think before she spoke. Listen. Get the information. And avoid giving Peyton O'Reilly any reason at all to suspect she was talking to a matchmaker.

Apprentice matchmaker.

On a suicide mission.

Ilsa must have lost her mind. Or else, Peyton's odd-couple parents were paying a premium price to have IF Enterprises locate a suitable match for their independent-minded daughter.

And of all the bad luck, the undercover work had to be done at the children's research center. Ainsley had protested that part, tried to convince Ilsa it would arouse less suspicion if she managed to bump into Peyton at the country club a few times. But Ilsa was adamant. Peyton was volunteering at the center. Ainsley could volunteer, too. Ilsa got the information she needed. The patients at the center got the benefit. Voilà, a perfect plan.

Perfect for whom? was what Ainsley would have liked to know. Because it wasn't a good plan for someone who was trying to avoid a certain someone else. And sure enough, from the minute she'd walked through the front doors of the center to begin her "volunteer" work, until now, a whole week later, she'd seen Peyton exactly three times. She'd seen Ivan ten times that often.

He was everywhere she went. In patients' rooms. In the administrative offices. In the lunchroom. In the hallways. He nodded when he saw her, but as often as not, he passed her without even knowing she was there. It hadn't taken even a month for the work to swallow him whole. She could see it in his face, in the weary lines around his mouth, in the purposeful way he moved, in the glint of satisfaction in his eyes. He was in his element, giving all he had every moment of every day and always on the lookout for the opportunity to do more.

She was nosy, and she snooped around, asking questions until she discovered he came in early and went home late. Every day. He'd taken off only one

day since the center opened, and she knew that because Matt had told her he had to insist that Ivan take
at least one day off to move into his new house. She
wondered what the house was like. Being nosy got
her the address, so she drove by it one day out of
curiosity.

It was a lovely house, two-story, with a wide front
porch, yellow frame, with white trim and a lawn of
manicured green. It looked comfortable, New England cozy, and—from the outside, anyway—like the
perfect place for a family. Ainsley wondered if he'd
thought of that when he'd chosen this particular
house, if he'd imagined children playing on the lawn,
a wife waiting for him on the porch, if he'd thought
that this would be a good place to call home, a comforting refuge to return to at the end of a long day.
And somehow, she knew that he had considered all
those things.

It was undoubtedly true that Ivan would always
give too much of himself away. But seeing this house
made her realize he would never desert the family
who would live there with him. His unselfishness
would extend to his wife and children, too. They
would be equal partners with him in his mission, another reason for him to give his best, his utmost effort
every day. His dedication was one of the things she'd
always admired about him, worried about for him, but
now she understood that whatever time and energy he

gave to the work of the Foundation nourished his soul, made him the man she'd fallen in love with.

As her car idled in his driveway, she imagined the way the house would be if she lived there with him. She freely admitted that she wanted to sit on the porch, to walk through the rooms...and yes, to be in the bedroom, waiting for Ivan to seek the love and passion he would find within her embrace. In all her life, she'd never known such yearning as she felt now.

And because of her—the apprentice matchmaker—the man she loved, the life she wanted, would be Miranda's.

Ainsley knew she had to talk to him, to apologize again for that impetuous kiss, and ask him if he would please forget it had ever happened and give her a second chance at being his friend. It wasn't at all what she wanted, but it seemed now the best resolution she could hope for.

But even with the decision made, finding the opportunity—the *right* opportunity—wasn't that easy. Despite the time she was spending at the center, despite seeing him on a regular basis, there was never a good moment to say "Hey, can we talk?", never a chance to pull him aside and say the words she had practiced over and over in her head. Any number of times, she'd buoyed her courage, lifted her chin, and set out determined to carry out her mission. But each time, she found herself with words hovering on her lips and no one there to hear them.

It wasn't that he spun on his heel and walked in the opposite direction whenever he caught sight of her. It was more like he wasn't even aware she was there.

IVAN KNEW she was there.

How could he not know when every fiber of his being went on alert practically the very minute she walked through the front door?

He had no idea how Ilsa had arranged for Ainsley to spend so much time at the center or what excuse she'd given. But he knew he couldn't talk to her. Not yet. Ilsa had cautioned him to keep his distance, to let Ainsley see him, but to avoid having any but the most trivial conversation with her. It was crucial, Ilsa said, that he be the one to choose the time and place for their *introduction of possibilities,* and the inevitable heart to heart. But before that could happen, Ainsley needed to have had plenty of opportunity to be close enough to realize how much she missed him.

Ivan could hardly stand the waiting, but he was putting all his faith in his matchmaker, following her advice to the letter, and hoping with all his heart she was right.

"I'M NOT DOING IT!" Jett, blond wig jiggling, was in fine form for her afternoon performance. "I'm not! And you can't make me!"

"Now, Jett," Hugh drawled in his sing-song and

rambling way. "You know you gotta do your exercising. You gotta work with your physical therapist."

"I don't want to," Jett said stubbornly.

"Wellll…," Hugh drew the word into a long pause. "I think you're gonna have to."

Jett pouted, pursing her movie-star lips. Then she turned toward the audience with a conspiratorial whisper, "Watch this. He won't know what hit him." Then, turning back to poor, dumb Hugh—the puppet with stuffing for brains—she batted her extra long, very flirty eyelashes. "Why don't *you* do the work for me, Hughie? I'll give you my dessert…."

Ivan stopped in the doorway, caught as he always was by the ingenuity of the puppets' design and by how real they sometimes seemed. The theater room was a hit. Sometimes the puppet shows were staged by patients, sometimes by family members, but there was usually a good-size audience, with staff dropping in as they could to catch the skits.

It amazed Ivan, whenever he chanced to see them in action, how the puppets seemed to stay in character. Jett was always the manipulator. Hugh always the dupe. No matter who was behind the scenes acting out the parts. Jett could say she hated her therapist, convince Hugh to do her therapy for her, and everyone laughed at her silliness. Whether the skit dealt with friendship or an imaginary game of football, or even the fear of dying, the puppets expressed feelings that individuals had troubles with. That, perhaps, was the best thing about them.

And Ivan knew he had Ainsley to thank.

The little gathering of patients and aides laughed, and it was only when he heard Ainsley's laughter that Ivan realized he was standing right behind her. He hadn't even noticed her leaning there against the wall, watching the skit from just inside the doorway. His heart jerked to attention and thudded so hard against his ribs, he thought everyone in the room must be able to hear it. He should go, slip out before she was aware he was there, but he lingered, breathing in the sweet fruity scent of her hair, imagining how it would feel to brush his fingertip across her cheek, remembering the warm taste of her mouth.

He must go. Make a seamless escape. Do exactly what he'd been doing for over a week. Wait until his matchmaker advised him the time for possibilities had arrived.

But then Ainsley, as if sensing his presence, looked back and saw him and his heart stopped at the wistful yearning in her incredibly blue eyes. "Ivan," she whispered, her voice full of longing, hinging on the edge of a question.

And it was too late. He couldn't just leave. But he said nothing, withholding the betraying murmur of her name, and just looked at her, knowing he had to make an excuse, had to get away before he ruined all of Ilsa's careful planning.

"The puppets are a hit," he said softly, not wanting to attract the attention of anyone else in the room.

"Yes," she agreed, the word little more than a sigh. "Ivan, could I...would you, please...?" She paused, and the tip of her tongue darted out to moisten her lips. "Please, can I talk to you?"

He could hear Ilsa's voice in his head. *Wait. Wait.* "I, uh, have to...see a patient. It's..." He didn't know what it was, but suddenly, his excuse seemed a moot point as her palm flattened against his chest and propelled him out of the doorway and into the hall.

"Look, I've been trying to talk to you for weeks," she said, her voice low, shaky with nerves, but intense. "And this isn't going to be easy to say because I know I ruined everything, but you have to let me say this before that one thing gets to be this huge, big thing, like that rhyme about the horseshoe and the nail and the whole war being lost, so that there's no chance of anything ever being right again, and I can't keep working up my courage to do this and then not getting even close to being able to say it and..." She brought the frantic rush of words to a halt and blinked rapidly to keep from crying. "The thing is, Ivan, I'm sorry I kissed you, but if you're going to be my brother-in-law we can't not speak to each other for the rest of our lives."

He was trying to process what she'd said, but just then the puppet show ended and people began filtering out into the hall. She didn't take her eyes off of him—probably afraid he'd disappear down the corridor if she did—while she nudged him farther along the hall and into the waiting room, away from the dispersing audience. It was late afternoon, nearly dinner time, and the waiting area was practically deserted except for a couple of adults and a teenager in the back corner. "Did you hear what I said?" Ainsley asked, moving from tears to a stalwart determination that she needed to finally have this discussion behind her. "You can't not talk to me, Ivan. And you can't keep avoiding me, either. I...I won't let you."

He blinked, surprised by her sudden forcefulness, astonished by what he thought he'd heard her say. "You're sorry *you* kissed *me?*" he said, sounding a lot like poor, dumb Hughie in his own ears. "But I kissed *you.*"

She rolled her eyes. "Well, yes, but I didn't give you much of a choice, did I? And then it got all out of hand and I got carried away with...with...well, with *feelings* I didn't know I had and I know it was stupid and I've regretted it ever since, but you wouldn't talk to me and I know it ruined our friendship and..." She let out a rough sigh. "Yes, Ivan, yes. *I'm* sorry and if you won't forgive me once and for all, I'm going to...to...to be sorry for the rest of my life."

His heart nearly leaped out of his chest. He couldn't believe it. She thought *she'd* ruined their friendship. She was sorry because *she'd* gotten carried away with *feelings* she hadn't known she had. She wanted *him* to forgive *her*.

"Well, I didn't think you'd be smiling like a fool right now," she said, sounding a bit unsettled by his sudden grin. "I mean, accepting an apology is normally a pretty serious moment for most people."

He laughed once more, letting the joy work its way out in a throaty rumble. "Oh, Ainsley," he said. "I do love you." And picking her up, he whirled her around and around in the second-floor waiting room under the watchful, wide eyes of the funny, furry creatures she'd painted on the murals. She didn't protest his joyous response, probably thought he'd lost his mind…but no, he'd only lost his heart to adorable, wonderful, mixed-up Ainsley. She couldn't know what he was so happy about. Not yet. But he wanted to hold it—hold *her*—for a moment out of time while this was all new and all the possibilities were falling into place. Ilsa had been right. The *introduction of possibilities* had happened…and neither he nor Ainsley had recognized it for what it was. They'd jumped to the same conclusion—that the kiss signaled the end of their relationship…instead of the beginning.

Setting her feet back on the floor, he kept his hands at her shoulders and smiled down at her. "*I* kissed *you* with feelings I was only beginning to be aware of," he said. "And I thought *I'd* ruined everything.

I've been trying to work up my courage to offer *you* an apology.''

She blinked and smiled, understanding more quickly than he had. "You mean, you thought I was upset because you kissed me and I thought you were upset because I kissed you, and neither one of us was really upset because we kissed each other?''

He thought that was it in a nutshell. "I think that pretty well sums it up except for the possibilities those feelings introduced.''

She blinked. "You think that was an...an *introduction of possibilities*...for you and *me?*''

"What else, Ainsley?'' His smile settled into a sweet certainty. "I've been having these funny feelings ever since I saw you that first day in your office. I wasn't certain until you kissed me that it was love.''

"*You* kissed *me*,'' she corrected with a return of the sassy attitude he loved.

"And was sure you'd never forgive me for it.''

"I thought I'd embarrassed you something awful. And then I missed you so much.''

"That was Ilsa's idea.''

"*Ilsa* was in on this?''

He nodded. "I had to bring in an ace on this, Ainsley, so I hired her as my matchmaker. As *our* matchmaker.''

"And she didn't even tell me?''

"She's very discreet.''

"Don't I know it. I never even suspected when she

sent me to the center to…'' She bit back the rest of the sentence, her eyes widening, and Ivan suspected she'd been about to spill a secret. But then her gaze turned accusing. ''You wouldn't speak to me, either. That was *her* idea, wasn't it?''

''She said you needed time to realize I was more to you than an extra brother, more than a friend. Maybe she thought we both had to be miserable apart before we could confront the possibility that we were meant to be together. She did tell me she'd had an idea from the start that we were a perfect match.''

Her brow furrowed. ''But I was so sure you'd fall in love with Miranda,'' she said. ''I'm a matchmaker. I'm supposed to know these things.''

''You're an apprentice matchmaker,'' he confirmed. ''And while I'm sure you're very good at forecasting who's most likely to fall in love with whom, you've got to leave a little bit of maneuvering room for other possibilities.''

She looked up at him, her eyes misting with hope and joy. ''You're sure you wouldn't rather have Miranda?''

He cupped her face in his hands, thrilled at the possibilities doubling and tripling right before his eyes. ''Positive. She wouldn't have me on a bet…which works out amazingly well since I feel the same way about her. I'm crazy in love with you, Ainsley. Can't you see that?''

Ainsley bit her lower lip, trying to hide its quivering. "But I'm not like her...."

"No," he agreed. "You're everything I want in a woman, everything I could ever hope to have in a wife."

"A...a *wife?*"

"We have a lot of possibilities to explore, Ainsley, and while I know you may not be ready to marry me just yet, I think it's only fair to warn you that I mean for us to spend the rest of our lives together. Starting now."

She looped her hands around his neck. "You sound pretty certain of yourself, Doctor. Personally, I'd be easier to convince if there was a little less talk in your bedside manner and a whole lot more..."

He cut off her words with action and a kiss that introduced a whole new world of possibilities.

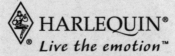

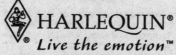

If you enjoyed what you just read,
then we've got an offer you can't resist!

Take 2 bestselling love stories FREE!

Plus get a FREE surprise gift!

Single Father

**He's a man on his own, trying to raise his children.
Sometimes he gets things right.
Sometimes he needs a little help....**

In March, look for

The Wrong Man
by Laura Abbot
(Harlequin Superromance #1191)

Trent Baker and his daughter
Kylie have come home to
Montana. Trent hopes the
move will help Kylie—and
him—cope with the death of
her mother. What he doesn't
expect is the complication
that occurs when Kylie's new
teacher turns out to be
Libby Cameron, the woman
who blindsided him with a
divorce twelve years before.

And in April, look for
Mommy Said Goodbye by Janice Kay Johnson
(Harlequin Superromance #1197)

What would you think if one day your wife disappeared, and everyone
believed you were responsible? And how would you feel if the only
thing that kept you from being arrested was your child's insistence
that his mommy told him she was leaving? And what would you do
if you suspected your son was lying?

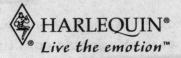

Visit us at www.eHarlequin.com   HSRSF1

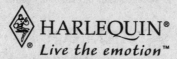

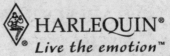